D.K. JOHNSON

StarChild

A Novel of Contact

First published by Amazon 2021

Copyright © 2021 by D.K. Johnson

All rights reserved. No part of this publication may be reproduced, stored or transmitted in any form or by any means, electronic, mechanical, photocopying, recording, scanning, or otherwise without written permission from the publisher. It is illegal to copy this book, post it to a website, or distribute it by any other means without permission.

This novel is entirely a work of fiction. The names, characters and incidents portrayed in it are the work of the author's imagination. Any resemblance to actual persons, living or dead, events or localities is entirely coincidental.

D.K. Johnson asserts the moral right to be identified as the author of this work.

D.K. Johnson has no responsibility for the persistence or accuracy of URLs for external or third-party Internet Websites referred to in this publication and does not guarantee that any content on such Websites is, or will remain, accurate or appropriate.

Designations used by companies to distinguish their products are often claimed as trademarks. All brand names and product names used in this book and on its cover are trade names, service marks, trademarks and registered trademarks of their respective owners. The publishers and the book are not associated with any product or vendor mentioned in this book. None of the companies referenced within the book have endorsed the book.

First edition

This book was professionally typeset on Reedsy.
Find out more at reedsy.com

Contents

Acknowledgement v

I Part One

Chapter 1	3
Chapter 2	11
Chapter 3	21
Chapter 4	31
Chapter 5	40

II Part Two

Chapter 6	47
Chapter 7	57
Chapter 8	62
Chapter 9	72
Chapter 10	87
Chapter 11	91
Chapter 12	97
Chapter 13	108
Chapter 14	117
Chapter 15	130

III   Part Three

Chapter 16	137
Chapter 17	141
Chapter 18	152
Chapter 19	163
Chapter 20	169
Chapter 21	174
Chapter 22	179
Chapter 23	184
Chapter 24	190
Chapter 25	201
Epilogue	208

Acknowledgement

No artist creates in a void. There are other people involved in any creative undertaking, some witting, many unwitting. In any research of alien abductees/experiencers, one soon discovers that many share similar experiences. I'd like to thank all the experiencers whose stories I've heard, some of which influenced this work of fiction. It takes rare courage to risk reputation and the love of family and friends to tell your truth. Many authors have also contributed to my knowledge of the subject. And not a few song writers have attributed otherworldly entities as a source of inspiration for their craft. I've tried to include titles of influential texts and songs in the body of the novel in hopes that readers will feel compelled to consult those books for more information and listen to the music with a new appreciation. It is a way of thanking those creators for edifying me.

I

Part One

One night in Joshua Tree

Chapter 1

"In space no one can hear you scream," cautioned the tagline for *Alien*, a blockbuster science fiction movie of the 1970s.

But it is not true.

Oh, technically it is accurate; the vacuum of space has no atmosphere composed of molecules to carry sound waves from mouth to ear. In fact, two unprotected humans would not last much longer than it took for their mouths to form that first exclamation of surprise before their eyes clouded, their lungs burst, and nitrogen gas boiled out of their blood, rendering further communication moot.

On the other hand, the catchphrase is *not* true because the predominant mode of communication in the universe is *not* via sound waves but via *thought,* and no mind is immune to, nor physical medium necessary for, telepathic transmissions.

Though Professor Daniel James never heard the alien messages screaming in his ears, once he realized nonhuman beings' thoughts were manifesting inside his head, the effect was as if they had stood beside him and bellowed sound waves onto his ear drums.

But let us start at the beginning.

On a LED screen before us is an image of the vastness of

space where shines a bright point of light, Teegarden's Star, a red dwarf in the constellation Ares. As the camera zooms in the scene resolves into a system of planets; we close on one, Teegarden's B, until the star's red globe nearly fills the screen and the small planetary disk that hangs beside it. A measured scholarly male voice speaks:

"Habitable exoplanets are the Holy Grail in the search for extraterrestrial life."

As the camera zooms closer the planet grows larger and larger until a bright halo appears, the atmosphere.

Our narrator continues, *"Direct imaging of atmospheres for bio-indicators: oxygen, carbon dioxide, ozone, and water vapor can tell us if a planet supports life."*

Moving closer still reveals a red-tinged sky with clouds and a surface of water.

"'Are we alone?' Mankind has taken a giant leap toward answering that question with a new era of astronomy."

Reversing its trajectory, our camera pulls back until Teegarden's Star is just another bright light in the firmament then pans to two impressive, unmanned spacecraft.

"Advanced space telescopes."

The larger, a reflector with 18 brilliantly shining gold hexagonal mirrors mounted perpendicularly on what looks like a platform of stacked fabric kites.

"The James Webb Space Telescope is our newest tool to study the cosmos. But that's not all..."

Panning to the smaller craft reveals a refractor-type telescope resembling a giant SLR camera with a long telephoto lens.

"Its companion THEIA is a valuable addition to the giant Webb."

On screen our grand tour now picks up, proceeding beyond

the two spacecraft, past the Moon to Earth where we stop to admire a beautiful shot of the Big Blue Marble; we then zoom in successively to North America, the West Coast of the United States, a mountain range in Southern California, to… Palomar Mountain. From a panoramic shot of the Palomar Observatory complex centered on the main Hale Telescope dome we pivot and zoom in on the Greenway Visitor Center.

"Yes, the era of space exploration is an exciting time in astronomy, for together Webb and THEIA may at last find proof of alien life in the Universe."

Finally, the camera pulls back to reveal a large LED screen mounted on the wall and the video ends with the title "The Search for ET" frozen on the screen.

As the lights came up and the music faded a man in his mid-thirties rose to address the small crowd gathered around the famous Schmidt Telescope in the main room of the Palomar Museum. Along the left wall was a large group of Japanese tourists, many wearing souvenir T-shirts and baseball caps newly purchased from the adjacent bookstore. The rest of the crowd was composed of a mixture of blue collar and white-collar Americans.

Astronomer Daniel James, PhD, addressed the crowd. "As we have just seen, the Kepler Telescope surveyed over a half million stars and discovered more than 2600 planets outside our solar system before it ran out of fuel. But the vastly improved optics and advanced instrumentation of Webb and THEIA will enable humans to learn details about these and new exoplanets as never before. Perhaps we will finally answer that age-old question: Does life exist outside of planet Earth?"

The lecture ended to polite applause.

"Now I'd be happy to take your questions."

From the front of the room, an older Japanese man, the tour guide, raised his hand and spoke when Daniel acknowledged him. "Given the vast distances, so many light years, how would other civilizations ever get to us?"

"An excellent question and one of the conundrums to the argument of humans ever making ET contact. Einstein's Special Relativity places a speed limit on the universe at light speed, or 186,000 miles per second in a vacuum. But it also says physical matter can only approach light speed and never achieve it, for at the speed of light the mass of the traveling object becomes INFINITE! So, you can see the problem. A rocket ship carrying human beings to the stars, or alien beings coming here for that matter, can never achieve light speed. And at lower speeds it could take hundreds of years, if not thousands, to make the trip from the nearest stars … one way."

Professor James enjoyed this interaction, a chance to demonstrate how science could explain the universe and explode myths and misconceptions in the popular ken, especially around certain topics like extraterrestrial visitation. As a man of science, he was an eternal skeptic, his duty to truth was consummate, and though as a youth he had been raised Protestant, he'd never really accepted the fantastical stories, the belief in the unseen, that formed the basis of Christianity, and indeed most religions. Observed reality, even when he was a child did not comport with the realm of faith. In science, the simple rule was if it can't be measured, it doesn't exist.

Another hand rose in the back, and Daniel quickly acknowledged it.

"If it's impossible to get here, what do you say to the experts on shows like Ancient Astronauts that say we've been visited by spacemen throughout earth's history?"

Another audience member piped up. "Yeah, I watch that show. They said the Great Pyramid was built by extraterrestrials."

"You're referring to UFOs and aliens?" Professor James chuckled. "Folks, that is fiction masquerading as science. In real science there is no room for theories unsupported by evidence."

Undeterred, the questioner continued, "What about Roswell? A crashed flying saucer and bodies. Wasn't that evidence?"

Dr. James, of course, had heard this argument before citing the most famous legend of UFO contact in modern history, and was ready. "That's been explained by the Air Force as nothing more than a misidentified high-altitude balloon and crash dummies," he said with a dismissive wave of his hand.

The whole crowd roared at that one. Sprinkled comments were heard like "They want us to believe that crap?"

Daniel was shocked at the strong audience reaction, which seemed to indicate that popular TV pseudo authorities were winning the war with scientific fact. He was proud of his identity as a debunker of popular misconceptions, especially in the realm of UFOs and aliens, a particularly fertile ground for myth-busting. But he quickly surmised he had few rational allies in this crowd and his irritation now showed. "I'll take one more question," he snapped.

"Professor, you ever see anything in the sky you couldn't explain?"

Relieved at the opportunity to bring the conversation back "to earth," Daniel became professorial again. "In all my years of studying the night sky, I've never seen anything that wasn't a natural or manmade phenomenon."

"Would you admit it if you did?" sneered another audience member, which got an echoing rise out of the crowd.

Daniel bristled at the attack on his authority. Science was sacrosanct to him, especially in such matters of pseudoscience or outright fiction. No one had ever presented *any* credible evidence of unidentified flying objects of extraterrestrial origin. He felt like his predecessor in the field, astronomer Carl Sagan, who famously said "Extraordinary claims require extraordinary evidence."

To him there was no legitimate evidence, let alone extraordinary, outside of bogus conspiracy theories pumped up by the tabloids and spurious TV shows, the likes of which had just been referenced.

When the audience continued to waste his time with their infantile arguments for unsubstantiated "facts," he finally lost his tenuous composure completely. "I deal in facts, not Big Foot and Little Green Men!" he bellowed, a little too forcefully, then caught himself and lowered his voice. "I don't waste my time on childish fantasies…nor should you."

The audience collectively groaned, and there were even a few scattered boos. The lecture was over and as a body they moved toward the door; only scattered applause was heard.

Emblazoned on the T-shirts of several of the Japanese tourists was the cryptic phrase "Adamski Lives!"

From the back of the pack a co-worker Siddhartha Sharma, an Indian man about Daniel's age, joined Daniel, mocking him, arms extended forward in the "Pelosi clap." Sidd greeted Daniel, his voice dripping with irony, "That went well."

"People are so gullible. Can you believe the crap they'll believe?"

"Yeah, the thing is, Danny, in a PR event you oughta leave'em laughin'...or at least *not* booing."

"I won't indulge that kind of nonsense."

"Just toss it off, hey, water-duck's back...and not a good idea to insult them. You never know who's in an audience." With that, Sidd's cellphone pinged and he paused to check the text message as Daniel began to pack up his lecture materials.

Suddenly hyper-animated, Sidd yelled, "Buddy! I just got the text! Deepa started her contractions!"

"Man, that's great! You're gonna be a papa!" They hugged it out. While Daniel was genuinely happy for his friend, his demeanor also betrayed a hint of envy. They started toward the exit; the news had energized them both and now quickened their pace. "And I'm guessing you won't be going to Joshua Tree."

"Sorry to bow out at literally the last minute."

"Don't worry about the hike. I don't mind going alone."

They walked out of the building and into the parking lot.

"You know I hate to miss it. There's no one else you can take?" asked Sidd.

"Not on this short notice. I'll be fine. You just get Deepa to the hospital before the blessed event. No birthing in the back of your pickup."

"Have I ever been known to cut things close?"

"Present situation excepted, but have you ever been on time for anything in your life?"

"Ah, my reputation trails me."

They reached Daniel's red Polestar Precept. Daniel opened the front trunk, which was bulging with travel bags, pulled out a duffle bag and plopped it on the asphalt at Sidd's feet. Sidd grabbed a knapsack.

"So close, huh?" said Daniel in mock lamentation.

Sidd tossed the knapsack into the white Ford F-150 pickup truck backed in the slot beside Daniel and quickly reached for the duffle bag.

"What if I'd got the call after we got to Joshua Tree?" Sidd reasoned, tossing the bag into the bed also. He opened the cab door and climbed in, pausing before closing the door. "Be careful out there alone. That high desert is unforgiving even in November. I know service is spotty but try to stay in cellphone range."

Daniel nodded and closed the trunk.

"Give Dee my best …"

"Will do. Melanie is with her now."

Sidd paused for a reaction but did not get one. "I'll make it up to you some way, buddy," he said while slamming the door and starting the engine.

Daniel shouted back, "Daniel's a great name for your kid!"

Sidd had pulled out but stopped to reply through his open window, smiling broadly. "Yeah, we're thinking more Hindi, you know, less Hebrew prophet."

Daniel laughed and waved goodbye as Sidd gunned his engine and exited in a roar of internal combustion.

In contrast, Daniel climbed in his car, energized the Polestar's electric motor, and quietly hummed out of the parking lot down the winding mountain road.

Chapter 2

Daniel was in love with driving again. Not since he'd owned his first sports car in college, that Austin Healy 3000 Roadster, rescued and restored from a junkyard, had he enjoyed driving so much. It showed now in his self-satisfied smile as he easily negotiated the curves and switchbacks of South Grade Road down Palomar Mountain.

In his choice of personal auto Daniel liked to think he was making an astronomer's statement about care of the Earth. Besides the obvious connection the Polestar name made to the heavens above, no other car on the market, EV or hybrid, was designed and built with such sustainability in mind. Given the ecological benefit of an all-electric vehicle, the interior uniquely utilized green materials, flax fabric, recycled plastic bottles and recycled cork vinyl to reduce vibration and weight by 50% without compromising luxury. Though the price was an extravagance on a staff scientist's salary, he'd nevertheless convinced his wife, Melanie, that the Precept was good for them…and the Earth. In the end she had agreed with his decision on principle, though his gift of a cute little RAV4 Hybrid helped a bit.

The Polestar wound through scenes of iconic Southern California terrain: Cleveland National Forest, Temecula wine country, Murrieta Hot Springs, Riverside, snowy peaks of San Jacinto and San Gorgonio Mountains, windmill banks of Palm Springs, and finally to the high Mojave Desert at Joshua Tree.

Daniel parked his Polestar next to Campbell House, the historic two-story stone bed and breakfast in 29 Palms, CA. Climbing out, he surveyed the grounds with an air of familiarity, breathing deeply of the fresh breeze that rustled the massive fan palm trees. He grabbed his duffle bag out of the front boot and entered a small white cottage on the manicured grounds in the shade of a quaint old wooden water tower.

Curled up on her living room couch watching the news, Melanie James, Daniel's wife, thirtyish, toned and the picture of wholesomeness, heard her ringtone and snatched her phone off the end table.

Jesse, a Golden Labrador sleeping at her feet, perked up. Seeing it was Daniel she answered, "Are you there?"

"Yeah, no traffic to speak of. Are you with Dee?"

"No, I'm home. Sidd will call me when he takes her to the hospital."

"You met with your lawyer today?"

"Uhuh."

After a long exasperating pause, Daniel finally broke the ice. "Well?"

"He doesn't want me talking to you, but I told him we want to settle this civilly."

"Good, maybe I won't need to get a lawyer. Where's Jesse?"

"Oh, he's here, waiting. Probably hears your voice."

Melanie put her phone on speaker and held it down to Jesse, a routine action she'd done so many times before that it now was an unspoken ritual every time Daniel was away from home.

CHAPTER 2

"Hello, buddy! How's my big boy? Miss me?"

Jesse barked excitedly at the phone, as Daniel continued making baby talk to him. Melanie laughed at their pet's antics, when, quick as a wink, Jesse bit down on the phone, snatching it out of Melanie's hand, and trotted away with it as if he had a new toy.

Melanie screamed, "Jesse, NO!"

Startled, Jesse dropped the phone and cowered. Melanie quickly retrieved her phone, then, down on her knees, wrapped her arms around her pet to comfort him. "Oh, it's alright, baby. Momma loves you."

Daniel was duly alarmed. "What happened?"

"Our baby boy tried to take custody of you."

"Maybe he could represent me."

Before Melanie could answer her phone buzzed and she noted the caller ID. "Sidd's calling. Gotta go."

Daniel yelled, "Keep me posted," before realizing it was to an empty line. Then, switching off his phone, he sat staring into space, feeling the sudden loneliness. Slowly he removed his wedding band as if testing the finality of what was coming, and his mind wandered back to an earlier time.

Daniel exited the elevator wearing a loose-fitting baseball jacket zippered up the front but bulging at his belly; his crossed arms cradled something underneath.

At the nurses' station a stern nurse looked up. Daniel smiled guiltily, alerting her suspicions.

Her officious authority had earned her the appellation of Nurse Ratched from Daniel in honor of the character from *One Flew Over the Cuckoo's Nest*. Going down the hall, he entered a room where Melanie sat in a hospital gown facing a window that looked out onto the limbs of an ancient oak tree. She looked depressed, as if bad news had been weighing on her. The room was festooned with flower bouquets. Daniel approached from behind, leaned down and kissed her cheek. "Mel, I have someone I want you to meet."

Without looking at him she responded dully. "Oh, who is it?"

"Well, actually, that's for you to decide."

He unzipped his jacket, pulled out a Golden Labrador puppy and plopped him on her lap. Instantly, Melanie's demeanor changed; she scooped the little gold bundle of energy into her arms. "Oh! He's beautiful!" She giggled like a kid as the puppy licked her face frantically as only puppies can do. "He's Jesse. Gotta be."

As Daniel sat on the windowsill nodding approvingly, the puppy was torn between them - who to go to? - until he saw a squirrel on the oak branch outside. Immediately, he began barking in a puppy soprano that carried easily through the quiet hospital hall.

"Oh, oh. Nurse Ratched is just down the hall," lamented Daniel as they scurried to hush him up. Daniel was caught still trying to stuff Jesse back into his jacket as nurse walked in.

She barked gruffly. "What's going on in here? A dog? You can't have animals in a hospital!"

"We were just leaving," said Daniel.

Holding Jesse before him and away from his now wet-with-pee T-shirt, he brushed by the frosty nurse. Daniel leaned into whisper, "We're all animals, nurse."

As she scowled back, on impulse Daniel held out the squirming pup, who promptly landed a big juicy lick right on nurse's lips. Melanie reflexively shrieked with glee as Daniel departed with the little Jesse James, kissing thief, leaving a sputtering and spitting nurse in his wake.

Back in the present, Daniel smiled at the memory of Jesse's stealth kiss and slipped the ring back on his finger.

The broad panorama of the desert landscape in Joshua Tree National Park spread out before him; sand, gravel, yucca and cholla cactus, and Joshua trees abounded. Majestic granite boulder stacks littered the land, making it a rock climber's paradise. Daniel walked up a broad alluvial fan, just another solitary hiker trudging up a wash. He stopped to remove his Pantropic felt fedora, mop his sweating brow, and survey the stark beauty around him. Only a soft wind and the solitary cry of a red-tailed hawk was heard. He continued up the wash when his cellphone suddenly rang. He uttered surprise to have service, but when he saw who was calling, he quickly answered.

"What is it, Melanie?"

"Daniel, you're disgusting!" she screamed.

"What's the matter?"

"Oh, don't play innocent. Wendy?" She spit out the name.

Daniel stopped, startled to silence, then composed himself and proceeded cautiously. "What do you mean?"

"Your girlfriend! That's what I mean."

"I…only just met her. She's hardly a girlfriend."

"Pleeeease, fucking in the storeroom of a shoe store? You're disgusting."

For a moment Daniel was utterly discombobulated, then he remembered his backpack and his notebook laying on the bed behind it. Did he? Quickly, Daniel checked the side pocket of his backpack. No notebook!

"Melanie, damn it! My journal is private! How dare you snoop around in it!"

"I'm your wife, Daniel! You have no secrets from me. And now I want the entire house… free and clear. Or do you want your little MARRIED girlfriend revealed in open court?"

"Don't you go there, Melanie! Melanie?"

Daniel frantically pressed phone buttons, but the call had dropped off. In utter frustration he screamed, "Now I lose service?" Cursing, he threw the phone down, and bent over, breathing in short gasps, hands on his knees. When the fit passed, he frantically picked the phone up out of the dirt and turned it on. The screen was cracked yet lit up. He sighed in relief. But it still read "No Service". Resigned, he proceeded up the wash.

Near the top were boulders he had to scale to reach the old dirt road that was his destination. Still muttering over the phone conversation, he blindly probed overhead for a handhold when he heard a tell-tale rattle. Coiled in the shadow of a large fissure was a southwest speckled rattlesnake, just a few feet from Daniel's bare hand. Reflexively, he jerked his hand back, lost balance and fell down several feet, landing awkwardly on his left foot, which collapsed and tumbled him to the ground. Hurt, he cried out, then lay immobile. After the initial pain subsided, he gingerly tried to stand but the ankle gave out and he fell again. Realizing he was seriously injured; he beat the sand with his fist in frustration.

When his fury was spent, he gravely considered the situation. Around him lay stark desert wilderness, an environment that had swallowed his cries like the maw of a vast whale. He checked his phone again; still it read "No Service." Daniel understood his dire circumstances. The likelihood of anyone happening upon him in this remote wash was miniscule. Somehow, no matter how painful it was to walk, he had to get to the old road.

From his backpack he pulled out a camera monopod, and, extending out its telescoped segments and locking them in place, used it as a crutch to stand up. Scanning the elevation above, he knew he must now go the long way around the boulders to finally reach the road and the easiest path back out to Hidden Valley Campground and his car.

Limping along, he tried not to put too much weight on the monopod, which, though solidly built, was meant to carry the weight of a 35 mm camera, not that of a full-grown man. For an hour he hopped along, leaving an odd trail of footprints and intermittent depressions and narrow furrows from the monopod "leg" in the sand behind him, a sign, he mused sardonically, that might confuse some hiker that crossed his path before the wind or, rain, erased it.

Winded and hot, but having finally gained his objective, he sat on a boulder and, without thinking, drank long from his backpack canteen. Thirst slaked for the moment, it donned on him that he should conserve resources in case he couldn't get back to his car today. He shook the canteen; the sloshing indicated there was not a lot left. Would it be enough?

Staring out at the high desert landscape, he mulled over his predicament and the events of the morning. How quickly his life had changed due to a simple omission, forgetting to pack his journal. Perhaps, subconsciously, he had wanted Melanie to find it and expose his guilt, forcing him to come clean about the brief, meaningless, affair. Or was it a twisted attempt to make his wife jealous? Despite their amiable "separation" of the last few months, he saw the landscape of his life without her as bleak and empty as the terrain before him. Mercifully, his mind drifted off again to a happier time.

Daniel, Sidd and Deepa Sharma, Sidd's wife, strolled among the exhibits in the Los Angeles Conscious Life Expo, booths with tables displaying New Age esoterica, crystals and other stones, essential oils, exotic clothing, psychic readers and healers, fantasy art of etheric beings, chakra singing bowls, didgeridoos and other strange instruments for creating music and "vibes" to cleanse and heal with subtle energies. It was a foreign culture to Daniel, the staid, rational scientist, and he observed the bizarre booths and strange people with the hauteur of one who held superior knowledge. What he witnessed only confirmed his worst prejudices against the soft, fuzzy thinking represented here. He'd been right to resist coming, and only regretted now that he'd finally given in.

Deepa had been after Sidd for months to convince Daniel to meet her friend Melanie. Finally, Sidd had agreed to be complicit in her matchmaking efforts and convinced Daniel to come along on the pretense that it would obligate him to nothing. They would casually drop by Melanie's booth and the two could check each other out. And, if "the moon was in the Seventh House and Jupiter aligned with Mars", then perhaps love would steer the stars - and lovers - to a match made…well, in heaven. Or not.

"I think Mel's booth is the next aisle over," Deepa said encouragingly, anxious for them to move along.

Daniel ignored her entreaty with the recalcitrance of the self-righteous. Passing by a booth called "Pyramid Power," he playfully donned an open, metal-framed, pyramid-headdress.

He grinned at them moronically, prompting Sidd to immediately snap a phone pic for posterity.

Aghast, Daniel cried, "Oh, God, Sidd. You didn't?"

"Yep, I did. Instagramming to the world. Astronomer Daniel James, PhD. Copy to the gang at Caltech, our new employer."

Daniel groaned. "Tell me again why this is a good idea."

Deepa quickly interjected before Sidd could respond. "You'll see, Danny. She's just the sweetest person."

"Yeah, buddy, a great personality." Sidd winked.

But Deepa had not missed his signal and elbowed him sharply in the ribs, effectively shutting Sidd up for the moment. "Sidd, she's cute and you know it."

Sidd grimaced from the "rib nudge." Momentarily speechless, he waggled his hand "so so."

Finally, they approached a booth named "Reiki Angels; Goddesses of Energy Healing" manned by several young women. One of them spied Deepa and hurried over to greet her. She was cute and bubbled personality but was plain with a plus-sized figure. Daniel's disappointment was apparent, and only confirmed that this whole outing had been, as he'd feared, a mistake. But, even so, he now gallantly stepped forward and solemnly offered his hand. "It's a pleasure to meet you, Melanie. I'm Daniel."

The young lady accepted his hand and curtsied in a slightly mocking gesture while suppressing an outright laugh at Daniel's stiff formality, registering her glee in a knowing glance to Deepa. "Oh! I'm not Melanie," the young lady exclaimed. "I'm Iris. Melanie stepped away for a moment." Then something drew her eye, and she continued, "In fact, she's right there."

Iris pointed behind Daniel where an attractive young woman

had just emerged from the crowd. Daniel turned to get his first look at a radiantly beaming Melanie…and was instantly smitten.

When I first saw you, I fell in love, and you smiled because you knew.

Chapter 3

Daniel snapped out of his reverie. With effort he rose to survey the empty valley below, dreading the long and painful trek out. As he stepped onto the undeveloped dirt road, washed out by decades of disuse and zero maintenance, his eyes were drawn down, where he was surprised to see fresh tire tracks. He could not be sure how old they were, there had been no rain to wash tracks away for months, but he sensed they might be new. And if the vehicle was still in sight, well, maybe it was a ride out for him. They led over a little hill just a few hundred feet behind where he was standing so, with little to lose, he limped on up; cresting the top, he was shocked to see a white minivan and two people sitting in a shaded campsite complete with tables, zero-gravity chairs, ice chests and gas grill. One, an older white man, wearing an Arizona State Sun Devils cap, waved him over. Daniel hobbled to the campsite.

The man greeted him. "Been waitin' on ya. Seen ya comin' up the wash earlier." He paused. "You hurt yourself?"

The other man, a Buddhist monk in a brown robe, tied at the waist with a cord, and sandals, serenely evaluated Daniel, saying nothing.

"My ankle's sprained," he tossed off casually, relieved now that his way out of a potentially serious dilemma was solved.

"Didn't expect to meet anyone up here. Pretty rough road for a street vehicle."

"Nah, know that trail like the back of my hand. Been comin' here for the last twenty-three years." He motioned to a folding chair. "Have a sit down, friend."

Daniel slipped off his backpack and settled into the chair under the welcome shade of a roll-out canopy attached to the side of the camper van.

"Cerveza?"

Daniel nodded gratefully. The man reached into an ice chest to hand him a frosty, dripping can of Modelo Especial. Daniel popped the tab and took a long, thirsty quaff, leaned back and relaxed. He let the cold amber liquid slake his parched mouth, creating a mildly pleasant brain freeze while the alcohol simultaneously cooled and warmed his throat and tummy. "Twenty-three years?"

"Yep, every November 20 you'll find the two of us right here rain or shine. Usually shine." He chuckled. "It is the desert." He offered his hand to Daniel. "I'm Byron."

Daniel shook it. "Daniel."

"Hoshi here comes all the way from Sendai, Japan."

Hoshi bowed his head slightly and Daniel reciprocated. "Sounds like dedication to a cause. What's so special about this neck of the desert?"

Byron beamed ear to ear, stood up and proudly pointed to a little hillock, a nondescript outcropping of rock and sand about 50 feet away. "Just over yonder is where man first met spaceman."

Daniel's bewilderment showed. "What do you mean?" He was suddenly concerned that maybe he had run into a pair of loonies.

CHAPTER 3

"You ever heard of George Adamski?"

Daniel shook his head warily.

"George Adamski was the first human being to contact an extraterrestrial being. The Space Brother Orthon landed his scout ship on that little rock and got out and shook Adamski's hand on November 20, 1952...'bout noon. And that's why Hoshi and me have been coming here for over two decades."

Daniel did not hide his dismay. "You believe that literally?"

This caused Hoshi to scrutinize Daniel even more intently, yet he maintained his silence.

Byron, however, was direct. "I take it you are an unbeliever, Daniel. What, may I ask, is your occupation?"

"I'm an astronomer...at Palomar Observatory," he said, a bit imperiously, hoping his identity as a fact-based professional would help quell the nonsense he was hearing.

Instead, Byron and Hoshi simultaneously voiced their surprise, and then Bryon laughed uproariously.

Daniel was confused as hell; this was not the reaction he expected. Seeing his consternation, Byron hastened to explain.

"Damnation! And you don't know?! Mount Palomar? That's where Adamski lived! George Adamski was an astronomer... and he photographed the first ever pictures of flying saucers, some of the best ever taken. And no one's been able to debunk them to this day."

Suddenly uncomfortable, Daniel stood, snatched up his backpack and swung it over his shoulder, eager to depart. "Well, thanks for the beer fellas. I need to be getting on the trail if I'm going to make it to my car by nightfall." But as soon as he stepped on his left ankle, it gave out and he fell to the ground. Both Byron and Hoshi rushed to help him back on his feet.

"Whoa there, fella. That is quite a bad wheel you got there," said Byron.

Daniel settled into his chair again, wincing at the sharp throbbing pain that was coursing through his leg.

Byron probed, "Where you parked? Hidden Valley?"

Daniel nodded. It seemed like a hundred miles off now.

"That's a good eight miles. You can't hobble that far. Looks like you're spending the night here, my friend. Hoshi and me will take you out when we break camp in the morning."

"But I'm not prepared for that," Daniel protested, his voice cracking. "And it'll be mighty cold tonight."

"We got an extra sleeping bag and mattress pad. Friend of mine cancelled at the last minute. And as far as food goes, we always bring way more than we need." Byron leaned back and smiled broadly. "Well, my friend, the skeptic astronomer, it must be fate. You're in for quite an education tonight."

"What education?"

"A little eyewitness education. Hoshi and me have been coming here for the last twenty-three years and have never failed to see UFOs."

Daniel chuckled derisively. "UFOs? Really?"

Byron did not take the bait; instead, his enthusiasm swelled. "Really! Sometimes motherships. And then…" his voice dropped conspiratorially "…there's the missing time."

"Missing time! What's that mean?"

Byron glanced knowingly at Hoshi. Hoshi pointed back at Byron, then spoke his first words to Daniel. "Imprant. Him. I see picture."

"Hoshi's English is a bit limited. He means implant. He's seen X-rays of the back of my head where I have a bullet-shaped implant, about the size of .30 caliber. No, I've never been shot.

And it's not metal, more like cartilage."

Daniel was immediately skeptical. "What did the doctor say it was?"

"He didn't want to talk about it. I was in the Air Force when they discovered it and, twice they paid for full body MRIs on me - and those babies are expensive - but they would never tell me what they found."

As he resigned himself to spending the night with his new companions, Daniel reluctantly settled in, rationalizing he might as well be the voice of reason for these strange men and their weird beliefs. "It could just be a naturally occurring function of the body. Like a cyst forms around a foreign object, say a bone chip from an old injury."

"Maybe," replied Byron, unconvinced. "They were always testing me for one thing or another. After one intelligence test, the doc looked at the results and said, 'This is good news for you.' I asked him what he was referring to and he said, 'Well, we know they won't kill you.'"

"What did he mean by that?" asked Daniel, alarmed.

Byron laughed. "He meant the Company doesn't kill people with a 160 IQ."

"The company?"

"The CIA."

"But you were in the Air Force?"

"The CIA calls the shots on a lot of this alien/UFO stuff."

"Still why would anyone want to kill you for having an implant, if that's what it is?"

Byron shrugged. "Maybe they just want to make sure you're not a Manchurian candidate for the other side?"

"Mind control? By aliens?"

"We do it to our own guys. Our government can program

people like in that movie where the assassin is going to kill the President. Only maybe it's not so easy if you're really smart. And they figure you can't be controlled by aliens either. I don't know."

"That is pretty far out, Byron."

"Tell me about it. There's been a lot of weirdness in my life that started when I was a kid. I was raised in the Pentecostal Church, where even a child could receive the Holy Spirit. We called it tarrying in prayer. You kneel at the alter saying 'hallelujah' over and over until you get it, the Holy Ghost. It can take many hours spread over days, sometimes weeks. But you wait and endure, all the while asking the Lord to bless you with his presence. I tarried from July of 1947 to February of 1948 twice every week. Well, one night in February while in a marathon praying service, I'd worked myself into quite a frenzy, trying so hard to get the Holy Spirit that I got hot and sweaty. So, I asked my mother if I could go outside and rest."

Outside young Byron swayed in a swing gazing at the starry sky overhead. He leaned back, eyes transfixed to the sky as a very bright star moved over his head and stopped, then descended to grow into a very bright sphere. While hovering over him, a white laser of light projected from the orb, fully engulfing the child, and rendering him immobile as if in a trance. Suddenly the laser switched off and the bright star swiftly rose straight up and disappeared. Young Byron, freed, rushed back down the stairs into the church to tell his mother.

"I'll never forget how calm she was and explained it was God telling me I was going to receive the Holy Spirit that night. I don't remember anything else from that night, but it's written in my Bible that I did get the Holy Spirit then and even spoke in tongues."

CHAPTER 3

It was late afternoon, and the shadows were long as the sun moved toward the western horizon. Byron tended to a portable barbecue that smoked with grilling hot dogs and hamburger patties. Hoshi took covered dishes out of a cooler and placed them on their small camp table, while Daniel sat with his injured leg extended before him. Draped over it was a blue ice pack that Byron had taken from one of their coolers to help reduce the swelling. Daniel was still thinking about Byron's story.

"The mind can play tricks on us, Byron. Any star that is stared at long enough will appear to move. And then the imagination of a child coupled with religious fervor can wreak havoc on reason. I know your memory tells you that you saw the star move and brighten, but stars just do not do that. Unless it becomes a supernova, an exploding star, and then it wouldn't have blinked out quickly. A supernova would have been visible for weeks, even months."

"You intellectual guys are always trying to explain things for us common folk." Byron was irritated by Daniel's condescending tone. "Like we shouldn't believe our own eyes." He flipped a patty then mashed it down with the spatula. The oozing fat that flamed up seemed to give him satisfaction. "Well, let me ask you this, professor, did you ever see *anything* in the sky you couldn't explain?"

Daniel paused to consider the question.

In the low hills of rural West Virginia, Young Daniel, a boy of eight, peered through the eyepiece of a small refractor telescope at a dark and starry sky. On a folding chair next to him lay a star chart, which he referred to using a flashlight covered with red cellophane secured with a rubber band, to keep his eyes adjusted to the dark, like a photographer uses a red light in a dark room while developing film. As he studied the chart, something just above the mountain ridge caught his peripheral vision. He looked up to see a bright orange fireball move slowly across the sky overhead, when another smaller orange orb emerged from the larger, moved quickly away and rushed toward him, growing larger and brighter. Then, in the blink of an eye, both objects just disappeared, leaving the small boy staring in wonder.

Daniel had never been able to adequately explain that sky anomaly of his youth, not even in all his years studying to become an astronomer and then practicing his profession. Gradually, the memory faded; he'd not thought of it in a decade or more. But now it all came back to him. How he'd excitedly rushed across the meadow, past the lone haystack, still wafting the fresh aroma of newly cut hay, to the two-story house of their small hollow farm to tell his mom what he'd just seen. His dad, who shared an interest in the sky and had bought him the telescope, as usual was gone, always on the road during weekdays, traveling his territory as a farm implement salesman. His mom, knowing nothing about the phenomena of the heavens, had briefly humored him and then returned to solving her crossword puzzle from the Charleston Gazette. Not even his model rocket club leader, the high school science teacher, seemed to understand the impact of the sighting on the young boy, dismissing it as a meteor that broke apart. For various reasons he knew it did not act like a meteor breakup, one being the secondary object that emerged traveled a path opposite the primary object, not like a bomb dropping from a plane carried the forward momentum of the plane for a time as it fell. This object moved away under its own power. Now though, he suddenly had to grapple with the possibility that he too had seen an unidentified flying object, shared a similar experience with a believer.... And he summarily rejected it.

Byron and Hoshi were both staring at him, waiting for an answer. Realizing he had spaced out a bit, Daniel snapped, "No."

"Damn, you're good or just don't get out much," joked Byron as he speared the hot dogs onto a plate with the hamburger patties. "Okay, boys, let's down these puppies."

Feeling ravishingly hungry now after the long day's ordeal, Daniel limped over to the camp table where the food was spread out. Hoshi politely bowed to Daniel, inviting him to step up first and fill a plate. As Daniel lifted a plastic plate, he disturbed a roach from the shadows. It darted at him, and Daniel was just about to smash it with the plate when Hoshi snapped, "Yamero!"

The force of Hoshi's voice was so commanding it stopped a startled Daniel's arm in midair. In the next instant Hoshi's demeanor returned to the humble monk again. He calmly stepped in front of a bemused Daniel, scooped up the insect in his hands and gently released it on the ground.

"Hoshi never kills anything," Byron explained. "And he's got me doin' the same thing. At home now I never even kill a ant."

After dinner, the boys relocated their chairs around a crude rock fire ring where Byron was building a fire with cut logs brought in by the campers. Daniel nursed a mug of hot coffee as the air cooled quickly with the setting of the autumn sun.

"So, you guys really think what you've seen out here all these years are flying saucers? There are all sorts of natural phenomena that look strange to people not familiar with the night sky: meteors, fireballs, ball lightning or just aircraft lights under unusual conditions can look other worldly."

Byron piled wood on the blaze which flared up sending

sparks high into the evening sky, black to the East but still red orange and deep blue in the West. Off to the East a single white star pulsed bright to dim. Hoshi watched it closely. "Not moving."

Daniel, too, had been following the object. "It is, but very slowly, relative to the fixed stars. Must be a plane heading to Palm Springs."

Fire duty accomplished, Byron joined them putting on a silly hat with blinking red lights front and rear. "I don't see no red navigation lights like a plane should have."

"Oh, they're there, faintly visible. But perhaps now you can appreciate my earlier point about mistaken identity. My eyes might be a little better than yours, especially for night vision. That unidentified flying object to you clearly identifies as an airplane to me."

"Okay, but that's nothing like the UFOs we've seen out here. Just wait. We'll make a believer out of you yet."

Chapter 4

The fire had burned down to glowing embers as the three talked on into the night. Byron was enjoying himself the most with a captive audience in Daniel and stories galore with which to regale him. Byron was a good storyteller, Daniel realized, so he really didn't mind his tales; he didn't agree with Byron's presentation of them as factual, but he found himself able to suspend judgment and just appreciate them as one might a good movie or novel.

"Back in the mid-eighties I was at the station house in Elkhart, Indiana on a slow Friday night when our dispatcher got a call of a UFO over a lady's house. He dispatched one car over there and was gonna tell another car to check it out, but I told him I wasn't doin' nothin', so I'd take it. When I got there the two officers were out, guns drawn on a large… scout ship, I'd say it was, hovering over the power lines. I think it might have been replenishing its batteries, or something like that."

"You're sure it wasn't swamp gas or ball lightning?" Daniel joked.

Byron took it good-naturedly. "That's alright, professor, but most people will believe a cop."

"Did you write up a report?"

"I'll get to that. Well, I got this message in my head,

telepathically I guess, from the beings in the ship to tell the two police not to shoot, so I told the boys to stand down with their weapons and I'd try to talk to them. We could see people of some sort through the windows of the thing. Then it began to glow red like an element in an electric stove and moved forward. I was afraid it was going to 'cook' the guys underneath, so I started to warn them. But when I reached into my black and white to turn on my PA, I hit the radar button by mistake and the thing took off like a bat outa hell. Well, we all jumped in our cars and pursued it across town and out into the country. I lost it for a while but then came over this little rise and there it was, like it was waiting on me. But then it took off right through a grove of oak trees like they weren't even there. Didn't damage the trees or the craft, like it was a ghost ship or something and then it just moved away at great speed.

I was all excited when I got back to the station house to make my report when the dispatcher got in my face, desperate like. He was screaming, 'Where you been?' And I said, 'What's the matter. I've only been gone for a half hour.' And he said 'Like hell. It's been two hours.' I looked up at the clock on the wall and he was right. He showed me the log entries where he'd been trying to radio me. I said, 'I didn't get nothing but static on the radio.' That was my first missing time experience."

His interested piqued, Daniel pressed Byron on documentation. "Could you show me a copy of your report?'"

Byron threw up his hands in exasperation. "There ain't none! Monday morning all of us were called into a meeting with some guys in dark suits, from the FBI or something. They told us that we are not to say a thing about this to anyone. 'It never happened,' they kept saying. I was standing in the back and ducked out before they got to me as I was scheduled to begin a week camping trip that day and I sensed this would muck things up for me if I stayed. When I got back, I was proved right. The police that had been on that call with me had all gone away for a week-long 'debriefing'. The FBI confiscated the logbook and all our reports. From that day on no one would ever talk about it. If I brought it up, they acted real scared and wouldn't answer. It was like it really never did happen."

Though impressed by Byron's vivid recall of an incident that was clearly important to him, Daniel nonetheless felt obligated to point out the problems for science. "But anecdotal stories are not proof, Byron. Credible though your story is - and you are sincere I'm sure - it's not proof of UFOs. Do you understand my reasoning?"

Byron just snorted and jabbed the embers with a stick. Hoshi, who'd been quiet during Byron's story, now pointed to Byron, "June."

Daniel was confused. "I'm sorry. I don't follow."

"Oh, he means I used to get abducted every June," replied Byron. "Yeah, I was still a cop in Indiana, and it seemed like every Spring, around June, I'd get taken by what they now call the Greys."

"Are you serious? What made you think you were abducted?"

"Lost time! Scoop marks on my body. Floating through walls and into a spaceship. All the classic stuff."

"Surely, they were just lucid dreams and insect bites you'd forgotten."

"You can believe what you want, professor, but I used to handcuff myself to the bedpost and sleep with my .45 beside me. You ain't takin' me!" He shouted, defiantly jabbing his fist to the heavens above, then laughed, shaking his head in resignation. "But if they want you, there's nothing you can do to stop it." Byron took the last of the logs and tossed it on the red embers.

Not willing to let Byron's explanation stand without a rebuttal, Daniel tried simple reason. "So, okay, let's assume for the sake of argument that abduction happens. What's the point? What can mere humans have that these superior, star-traveling beings, want?"

"Fair question. I've heard theories. One is that they're actually time travelers from our own future, where their people are dying out because they can't have babies. They want our DNA to make hybrids to save their race."

As the log burst into flames on the hot coals, Daniel pounced. "Now, they're time travelers, another concept just full of paradoxes!" He was on familiar ground again, the outlandish conspiracy theory that he loved to pepper with scientific fact and logical suppositions. "What happens if you go back in time and kill your own grandfather, huh? Logically, you would also kill yourself because you never could have been born!"

Daniel shook his head in dismay. "And telepathy? You said you got a message in your head from the space men! That's nutty talk, Byron. Another logical impossibility with no verifiable data. It most likely was your overactive imagination amped up by the excitement of the situation, certainly not mind-reading aliens." He sighed and checked his watch. "It's almost midnight and I'm really bushed. I need to get that sleeping bag out."

Neither Byron nor Hoshi spoke, and Daniel started to feel perhaps he'd been a little too harsh in his rebuttal. "Seems you boys wasted your time out here this year. Hope I didn't dampen your fun."

CHAPTER 4

Yet surprisingly Byron seemed unperturbed; he moved to the van and pulled out a rolled mattress pad and sleeping bag. "Ya see, the thing about the aliens is, it's always on their time."

He plopped the rolls down. Daniel saw his reasoned argument had had no effect on Byron, which always infuriated him. He had little tolerance for an ignorant oaf who couldn't see how clearly wrong they were in the face of logical fact. With such people Daniel quickly lost patience.

"Well, I'm here. So where are your damn UFOs?" he asked sarcastically.

Byron calmly went on. "When it's time for them to come, they'll be here. Right, Hoshi?"

Hoshi pointed to where he was intently watching a light in the West, which was glowing brightly as it moved just above the horizon. "Time. Now."

Daniel turned to look and immediately discounted the object. "That's just another of those planes like we saw before."

He had no more than finished his thought when the light suddenly stopped, brightened and like lightning streaked over them in a split second, disappearing to the East. Byron and Hoshi jumped into action.

"What the fuck was that?" cried Daniel. He was literally shocked. Nothing in his experience or knowledge base of sky phenomena could have accounted for what he just saw. A meteor was the only thing that could have come close to the speed of object, but the duration was much too long and had covered the entire arc of the sky from horizon to horizon. The longest meteor flamed out in a few degrees at most. No known jet aircraft, or rocket for that matter, could have done such a maneuver. Certainly, no manned craft. The g-forces from the instantaneous acceleration would have crushed a human being, or any animal, he was quite sure.

As he had done all his life when confronted with something unusual, that he couldn't immediately account for, he paused and considered the information rationally step by step. And invariably within a few minutes - or on rare occasions days - he'd come up with a logical explanation. Here, though he was completely stumped. Nothing in his personal experience or scientific training could explain this. And he feared his "education," as Byron had put it, was just beginning.

"Radio," Hoshi called to Byron, ignoring Daniel's outcry.

"I'm on it," responded Byron as he ran to the van and quickly pulled out a CB radio rigged and ready to go. He grabbed the mike and keyed it. Speaker feedback whined into the night air.

"What are you gonna do with that?" cried Daniel.

Byron was grinning from ear to ear. "I got this idea over the summer. Seems like it might help in communication. If this works, we're in for a fun time." With that Byron spoke into the mike. "Testing, one, two. Whoop tee doo. ET, comin' at ya on Channel 22."

"There!" Hoshi pointed to the North where two lights had suddenly appeared.

"Okay, ETs. Move forward." The two lights immediately started moving toward them. "Did you see that? Oh, this is gonna be fun, fun, fun. ET turn East, then back toward us, then fly straight over head."

Immediately the lights mimicked Byron's commands, stopping directly over their camp. Just two bright white lights were visible but obviously they were intelligently controlled.

"Change coror," Hoshi suggested.

"Great idea. ET turn red." No sooner said than done. The boys shouted their delight, as Daniel only stared in disbelief.

CHAPTER 4

"This cannot happen. It's impossible." Was all Daniel could say. A life of measured reasoning had convinced him the Universe, vast and complex though it was, was nonetheless explainable via physical law. Quantum mechanics created some bizarre behavior in objects on the subatomic level, where it was a given that the micro world was *different* from the macro-world. Newtonian physics and quantum physics did not mix and applied, both verified experimentally, in their respective realms. The great Albert Einstein had not found a successful GUT, Grand Unified Theory, and neither had any of the equally brilliant minds of science since.

But Byron was not thinking of GUTs; he was having a ball. "We could use more of these guys. What do you think, fellas, an even dozen?"

As he spoke ten more lights appeared out of nowhere. And they started to change color randomly. As Byron continued his directions, the sky was filled with colored lights, then they all moved toward the common center of the camp site. Daniel was transfixed, mesmerized by what he was witnessing. This went on for many minutes, the sky filled with multicolored lights until Byron could not keep up.

He put the mike down. But the orbs did not stop, they quickly formed up and continued to put on a grand show. Soon the three humans were yelling and cheering like schoolkids at the amazing aerial acrobatics they were witnessing. Even Daniel finally suspended his disbelief and got into the mood of the night, marveling with a childlike wonder at the orbs' antics.

Finally, as a finale, the moonless sky went black as the orbs shut down in unison. Hoshi, who seemed to know better than the others where to look, pointed to the West where astonishingly there were hundreds of orbs flying toward them.

Then the orbs shifted to form two giant bird wings spanning thousands of feet in either direction. The boys were beside themselves with glee.

But it was not over. The wings began to flap, like a real bird! They passed over and out of sight to the East. The sky went dark again, and the boys continued cheering, fists pumping, prancing up and down joyfully. Even Daniel, bad ankle and all, tried to join in. When their exuberance subsided, they finally could analyze what had just occurred.

Daniel was vociferous. "Are you kidding me?! It's impossible, what we just saw, impossible!"

"Professor, I don't know what you brung to the table, but that's the best show we've ever had!" exclaimed Byron.

"I cannot explain it, but I'll never doubt you guys again."

But Hoshi had not joined their postmortem yet; he gazed toward the large mountain to the East. "Not gone. Big."

He pointed; Byron and Daniel followed his gaze. From behind the mountain multiple lights rose slowly. More appeared and kept rising, revealing what looked like a giant Ferris wheel of multi-colored lights, the outline of a huge ship, a thousand feet across.

Daniel could only gape in awe. "Mother of God."

The giant mothership tilted toward them as it cleared the mountain peak, reducing everything beneath it to insignificance. As the majestic ship moved directly overhead, there was no sound and the entire hilltop was cast in an eerie otherworldly light like a prolonged lightning flash. Each man reacted differently to the reverence the ethereal ship commanded. Byron fell to his knees, arms spread "tarrying in prayer"; Hoshi slipped into a serene meditative trance; Daniel, inexplicably emotional, quietly wept.

CHAPTER 4

Then, abruptly, a piercing shriek rose out of the West, stabbing their eardrums with the pricks of a thousand pins.

And suddenly, the mothership was gone. It had blinked out as if it never were, just before 3 F-18 fighter jets with afterburners blazing, streaked across the empty sky above them. With no target, the jets broke off left, right, and straight up, defined by the long blue flames that drove them. After long turning arcs, they re-converged over the campground to streak in low, buzzing the small hill and forcing the boys to the ground with the concussive sound. Then, they, too, were gone, leaving a sky that seemed as void as the depths of space before the universe existed.

Chapter 5

The landscape gradually brightened with sunlight muted by the high clouds that had come in over the wee hours of the morning. A solitary prone figure lay completely encased in a sleeping bag near the smoldering white ash of the bonfire. Everything appeared lifeless until the dark form in the bag stirred to reveal a human head. Daniel stiffly stretched his aching body and crawled out along the ground to where his knapsack lay. He quickly checked his cellphone. It still read "No service."He looked like he was suffering the world's worst hangover, haggard, disheveled, and shivering in the cold November morning. He gazed longingly at the sky, nostalgic for last night's encounter. As he picked up the knapsack, he noticed his camera laying on the ground beside it. Did he? He quickly scooped it up and turned it on. The LED screen stayed black. The battery was dead. He turned to the van as he heard the sliding side door open. Out stepped Hoshi, followed by Byron. Nobody spoke the usual banalities of morning. Too much history had passed in the last 12 hours to put to words without time for processing.

Soon everyone was moving about, cleaning up from a quick breakfast of sliced ham, fried eggs, and untoasted white bread. Daniel had removed his hiking boot and took his sock off to reveal his badly swollen and bruised left ankle. Byron came over to examine it. "That looks bad. Best get yourself to the ER in Joshua Tree as soon as you get to town."

Grimacing, Daniel gingerly redonned the sock and shoe, and then asked one of so many questions that had been on his mind all morning.

"What happened to it? It just disappeared."

Byron thought for a moment before answering. "They don't operate in just three dimensions like us. I think it was still there, just phased out of our dimension into the next."

"Let's say I could even believe that. Why didn't the jets come with all the small ships?"

"I'm not sure those were actual ships. They're light orbs, something like our drones. I think their technology can control them like we do pixels on a computer screen."

Daniel turned away to consider that. Byron stared at him for a long beat then asked the inevitable question. "What will you do…now that you're in the 'club'?"

Daniel sighed. "Honestly, I don't know. If I value my career. Nothing." He paused thoughtfully. "If I value the truth…?"

They let the question hang between them until Byron moved off to help Hoshi pack the gear into the van. All was ready for departure when Hoshi sensed something again and pointed to the North, where low on the horizon a black object hovered. As they watched, it started to move toward them, gaining speed.

Daniel spoke first. "Is that another ship?"

Hoshi shook his head. "Miritary."

"Black ops military." Byron explained. "Time to leave."

As the others scrambled into the van, Daniel stood mesmerized by the object that now was revealed to be a helicopter, unmarked, flat black. It flew straight at them on a course of imminent impact and seemed to dip lower just before it reached the little hillock, an intimidating but risky maneuver that sent Daniel once again to the deck, face first, as it zoomed over less than 20 feet off the ground. As he rose to his knees, spitting sand, Daniel's eyes followed the retreating helicopter but then refocused on the ground before him. Curious, he leaned in closer to see in the loose sand all around the campsite dozens of *small humanoid footprints*.

The paved parking lot at Hidden Valley Campground was surrounded by massive boulder hills. Byron's white van came off the dirt trail from the desert and stopped at the lone vehicle parked there, Daniel's red Polestar Precept. Daniel emerged from the side door followed by Hoshi as Byron watched from the driver's seat. As the Buddhist monk stared at Daniel, his eyes carried a depth Daniel had not seen before. Silently, he pointed one finger to his own heart center, then toward the sky and finally touched the same finger to Daniel's chest over the heart chakra. Then Hoshi stepped back to honor him with the universal Buddhist sign of respect, the *Anjali mudra*, bowing with hands clasped together over the heart, fingers touching. Daniel tried his best to return the gesture. Hoshi climbed into the front passenger seat as Byron solemnly saluted and the van drove off, leaving Daniel alone in the empty lot.

High in the sky over Joshua Tree National Park a lone aircraft, too small and quiet to be noticed from the ground, had been slowly pacing the figures below. The black, unmarked MQ-9 Reaper military drone was a single black speck in the vast clear blue sky from that altitude, but its high-definition imaging cameras rendered all below into fine grained images that were quickly transmitted back to the operator's station somewhere in the United States.

Remote operation of unmanned drones was the future of surveillance in the military. Operations in war zones all over the world were conducted on the computer consoles of airmen in air-conditioned trailers outside of Las Vegas, Nevada. And on an operator's screen somewhere now appeared high definition images of 3 faces, images that were resolved in a matter of seconds to identities of the men below by sophisticated facial recognition software. There on a small screen-in-screen image overlaying the video of the Hidden Valley parking lot was a rendering of Daniel's photo ID from the California Institute of Technology.

II

Part Two

Lights that call me, move me, turn me to stone
Are taking, taking, taking me home.

Chapter 6

At a large wooden desk inside a lavishly appointed military brass office sat a graying and distinguished Air Force officer, Colonel McDonald, his paunch revealing years of privilege and soft duty. A knock on the door reverberated from the far end of the room, to which the colonel sharply replied. "Come!"

The door opened and Captain Rocco entered, likewise an Air Force officer though of middle age and carrying a large muscular frame. He strode confidently up to the colonel's desk and sat without saluting. Though the captain was of lower rank, one sensed equality *vis a vis* the colonel. Captain Rocco was quick to report. "Last night three F-18s were scrambled for a large radar target over the Mojave."

McDonald grunted indifferently, as if the report were routine. "How large?"

"The size of an aircraft carrier."

Suddenly interested, McDonald looked up, and chucked the document he had been sourly perusing. "Did we get visuals?"

"All gun cameras malfunctioned." McDonald's face registered his disappointment, as Rocco paused for effect. "But on the ground…there were witnesses."

McDonald perked up again. "Civilians?"

Rocco nodded.

"Contact?"

"We think so".

"IDs?"

"Two of no interest, a retired cop and a Japanese national. But one is a professor at Caltech now working at Palomar."

Colonel McDonald leaned back and rested his pudgy white hands on his ample belly. "Perhaps we could pay him a visit."

"On it as we speak."

With a self-satisfied smile, Colonel McDonald closed the report he had been reading. On the cover was the title, *Top Secret - Eyes Only. Extraterrestrial/Human Hybrid Breeding Program.*

Daniel, his left leg encased in a medical walking boot, relied heavily on a cane as he limped into the back entrance of the Hale Telescope building on Mount Palomar in Southern California. The drive home from Joshua Tree had been torturous with his left ankle unusable and throbbing the entire trip. Luckily most modern cars could be driven with one leg, the necessity of a "clutch leg," the left, obsolete with the advent of automatic transmissions. Electric cars were no different and had the added advantage of one often not even needing to use the brake pedal as lifting one's foot off the accelerator under most circumstances was enough to slow the vehicle. But it didn't change the fact that the nagging pain from his injured ankle was there for the whole journey. The emergency room physician had advised him to take only an over-the-counter Aleve for the swelling if he insisted on driving back that Sunday.

Then the confrontation with Melanie had not gone well. Though she hadn't thrown his clothes out in the front yard as immortalized in country songs, she had packed his suitcase and had it sitting in the foyer when he arrived, with the ultimatum that he drive on to their cabin in the mountains at Julian. After giving Jesse a quick hug, he was ushered out the door.

Though the Julian cabin was log, it was far from rustic, but the journey and the excitement of the previous night had exhausted him such that he plopped on the bed as soon as he walked in the door and was out like a light. A morning shower, fresh clothes and breakfast at a local cafe had him at least bodily ready to report for work, if not at his alert best.

In the data control room, he made his way to a desk and computer console, where he immediately signed in and began a web search. The subject was George Adamski. He quickly discovered that there was a plethora of material on the man, who had lived on Palomar Mountain, a place called Palomar Gardens that was now an RV campground on the South Grade Road that snaked its way up Palomar Mountain to the observatory, but most of the info was negative. Adamski was the first member of a group of disparate individuals known as "contactees," people, all men it seemed, that claimed in varying degrees to have had contact with beings from outer space. Adamski had written several books on his experiences, including the first *Flying Saucers Have Landed* which recounted his first contact in Joshua Tree National Park on the site of Saturday night's encounter. Most, if not all, of his books were best sellers in their day, the 1950s. Adamski himself had become a world-wide celebrity and spoke before large crowds of enthusiasts all over the world; he even claimed to have had an audience with the Pope at the Vatican. In Japan he was especially popular which helped explain Hoshi's lifelong interest as Byron had explained Saturday night. In fact, the reticent monk had once traveled to London to personally meet Adamski's coauthor, Desmond Leslie, a noted WWII aviator. But since space exploration was in its infancy and little was then known about even our solar system, which had only been explored via ground-based telescopes, the largest being the 200 inch Hale at Mount Palomar, the fantastic stories the contactees told of Venusians and Martians, who coincidentally looked just like modern Earthmen and women in futuristic cloths, did not pass the smell test of even a few decades before science caught up and facts debunked their tales.

But this was not to say Adamski, anyway, was a total fraud. He was a serious amateur astronomer; Daniel was impressed with his equipment, two reflector telescopes, one a mammoth 15 incher housed in its own permanent domed structure. His pictures of numerous "scout craft" and cigar-shaped "mother ships" had passed the scrutiny of the photographic community of the era, at least those who took the time to study them seriously, like movie mogul Cecil B. DeMille's cinematographer.

Daniel didn't really know how to judge Adamski's story. There were large, easy to poke holes in his narrative, as humans gained knowledge of our own solar system. For instance, the scorching, toxic atmosphere on Venus made an environment impossible for the existence of life as we knew it. To be fair, Adamski's Venusians claimed to live on the inside of the planet. But that too carried immense credibility issues.

No, in an earlier time Daniel would have quickly discounted Adamski's stories as the fantasies of a lunatic or the fabrications of a con man. That is, prior to his own experiences of last Saturday night.

So intent was his focus on Adamski's UFO pics on his

computer screen that Daniel didn't see Sidd come in behind him and was startled by Sidd's greeting. "Hey, buddy," he said casually until he saw the boot and cane. "What happened?"

"Oh, had a little accident."

"On your hike? Where?"

"Lost Horse Valley. But it was okay, a couple guys drove me out." Daniel pointed to the screen that displayed a series of black and white flying saucer photos. "Sidd, ever heard of George Adamski?"

"No, should I?"

"No. But he was an amateur astronomer that lived here on Palomar Mountain. He took these pictures. What do you think?"

"Flying saucers?" Sidd was cautious, wondering where this conversation was going. "What about 'em?"

"They're not fake, according to Cecil B. DeMille's cinematographer. See the atmospheric softening? Back in the 50s that was impossible to get with small scale models. And there was no Photoshop."

His impatience growing, Sidd pulled a pink "It's a Girl" bubble gum cigar out of his pocket and rapped Daniel on the head with it to get his attention.

"Hey! What!?" Daniel reacted from the unexpected blow, then, seeing the cigar, "Oh, crap, I'm so sorry, buddy. Congratulations!" With difficulty, Daniel stood up to embrace his friend. "How is the little one? And Dee? How's she doing. No complications?"

"Mom and bambino are fine. We have a little princess born Saturday night."

"A daughter? That's great. I'm so happy for you two."

After another perfunctory hug, Daniel returned to his

computer screen, obviously more interested in it right now. Sidd playfully interjected. "We named her…" He waited for a response from Daniel but did not get any and finally added a deflated, "…Kamala."

"That's great, buddy," was Daniel's preoccupied response. "Sidd, this guy Adamski claims to have been visited by ETs. And you know it happened right out there in Joshua Tree? Right where I was Saturday night."

An uncomfortable silence followed as Sidd tried to fathom his friend's distracted behavior. "Something new happen between you and Melanie?"

"This divorce thing isn't going so well," Daniel offered, vacuously.

"Thought you already had an agreement to share things equally?"

Daniel shrugged, "Melanie changed her mind, now she wants the house." He paused, then added, almost as an afterthought, "I've moved into the cabin for the time being."

"Say what?" Sidd's shock was genuine.

But Daniel continued undeterred. "This guy Adamski wrote several books on his ET encounters, and he actually had worldwide fame in the Fifties."

Sidd finally gave up and retreated to his desk. He was just sitting down when he saw Dr. Wolfgang Sauer, a man in his late sixties and their boss, enter the room. He turned back, hoping to warn his friend but had no chance as Dr. Sauer made straight for Daniel. Sidd quietly sat down anticipating what was coming.

Standing behind Daniel, Dr. Sauer saw the flying saucer pictures on the screen. He spoke with a heavy German accent. "What the hell are you doing, James? Flying saucers?"

Surprised and embarrassed, Daniel quickly shut down the monitor. "Oh, some research, sir…a local astron…guy."

But Sauer was not buying it. "Research? Maybe you should research public relations. I got a call this morning complaining about your lecture on Friday. Seems you insulted a friend of President Thomas and a Caltech alumnus."

"I just gave my usual talk."

"You all do your turn at public lectures. Why is it the complaints are only about you? Why can't you be more like Sidd here? No one ever mentions him."

Sidd grimaced at the dubious compliment. Daniel had no response. Sauer handed him a memo note card. "Here's the info on the man you insulted. Call him today and apologize." Sauer added, "Is the research schedule ready yet?"

"I'll have it finalized by day's end."

"I'll expect it on my desk then."

"Yessir."

"Good. And less recreational research, James."

Dr. Sauer abruptly pivoted and left the room. Sidd jumped up and, walking behind Daniel, leaned into whisper, "*Der fuehrer ist* peeved." Then Sidd was gone, fast on the heels of Dr. Sauer. "Sir? A word please?"

Daniel was just hanging up the phone as Sidd returned. "Have you done your penance?"

With a quizzical look, Daniel offered, "That was a bizarre conversation."

"How so?"

"Guy wants to have lunch this week."

"Like a date? What are you getting into?"

"No, no," he groaned at Sidd's homophobic innuendo. "He

sounds interesting, actually; retired physicist, knew Carl Sagan, consultant on a Spielberg film."

"Which one?"

"*E.T.*"

"Maybe he'll talk flying saucers with you." Sidd took a seat then nonchalantly tossed out. "Oh, *der fuehrer* is green lighting my Supermassive Black Hole Binaries proposal. FYI."

"I thought that was to be *our* P200 project?"

"You'll have to talk with him. He didn't mention you."

Daniel's expression said, "And you didn't bring it up?" But he shrugged it off. "Oh well. It doesn't matter. Congratulations."

At their log cabin in the woods near Julian, Daniel parked his Polestar beside the rustic structure. With cane and walking boot, he slowly climbed the few stairs to the covered porch in the front.

In the darkened living room, he flipped on the light switch and placed his briefcase on a small desk where sat an Amazon Echo. "Alexa, play music."

Alexa quickly responded in her sexy female, Siri-like, voice: "Here's a song I think you might like."

As Daniel started into the kitchen the device began playing David Bowie's "Star Man."

He stopped short, wheeling around. "How the fuck did you come up with that?" Then as he listened he chuckled at the apropos lyrics. "Too late, Bowie. Star man already blew my mind."

At that same moment as if in answer, he heard a pronounced cracking sound that seemed structural from the ceiling overhead. "Wind must have picked up," he reasoned.

He opened a cabinet to pull out a fry pan. In it a trapped

daddy-long-legs spider was frantically trying to get out but could not negotiate the slippery no stick surface. Daniel tore off a paper towel and started to kill the critter, but then stopped and instead stepped outside to deposit the insect on the back porch, where it quickly scampered off.

"Hoshi would approve," he concluded, chuckling to himself.

Later Daniel was in bed reading *Communion* by Whitley Strieber with its iconic alien face on the cover. Strieber, a successful horror novelist, had written, "A true Story" he claimed, about a series of encounters with Grey aliens at his log cabin in upstate New York. Daniel had not known much about the book, but the cover drew him in; the black teardrop shape of those alien eyes was mesmerizing. Whitley's experiences were full of dark terrors as his alien captors performed painful physical procedures on his body. Once, when he protested they did not have the right to operate on him, they surprised him by claiming that they absolutely did have the right to do what they wanted to him. But for some reason Daniel did not feel Strieber's abductions resonated with his experiences in Joshua Tree. He yawned, laid the book on the bedside table, laid back, closed his eyes, and ordered, "Alexa, bed light off." The light switched off.

He slept soundly. The digital clock at bedside read 4:11 AM, when suddenly a loud house shaking crash from the wall behind his headboard jolted Daniel awake. In alarm, he wondered, Did something hit the house? and bolted out of bed clad only in his boxer shorts. He dashed out of the bedroom and down the hall.

Through the front door and off the porch he leaped and started around the corner when his attention was drawn up to the night sky. He was stopped in his tracks by an amazing sight. Directly overhead was the constellation Orion with the half-moon shining above red Betelgeuse while underneath radiant Sirius sparkled. All were picture framed by white clouds as if held back by some invisible force. The individual stars and the moon were rimmed by distinct halos that made them appear much larger than they truly were. As Daniel marveled, a single wide swathed meteor slowly burned across his field of view.

He broke his reverie long enough to walk behind the cabin but could find no source for the noise. Clearly nothing obvious had struck the house. So, he hurriedly backtracked to the front clearing to see the spectacular sight again, but the clouds were already drifting in to obscure it. Nevertheless, he stood there shivering with the cold night air on his bare torso until the clouds had nearly covered the sky again.

As Daniel prepared to crawl back into bed, he saw the walking boot standing where he had left it at bedtime. He gaped at his bare left foot, shocked to realize he had been walking on it normally without pain.

Chapter 7

Down a long hospital corridor Daniel strode without the hint of a limp, carrying a bouquet vase of two dozen mixed roses. He entered Deepa's room where she was breast-feeding her daughter with Sidd standing beside her, lovingly caressing the little cherub's black hair. When she saw Daniel, Deepa modestly covered her breast with the blanket wrapped around her baby.

"Madonna and child! Dee, you look radiant, motherhood becomes you." He looked at Sidd. "And fatherhood you, my friend."

Deepa smiled sweetly. "Thank you, Danny. We've been wondering when we'd see you."

Sidd took the flowers. "Thank you, buddy. They're lovely," he said, sarcastically. "You dash into Trader Joe's on the way?"

Daniel laughed, "No, buddy. They're from an honest to God florist."

"Sidd, stop teasing!" Dee reprimanded him. "Danny, they're professionally done, as *anyone* can see."

Ignoring her, Sidd continued. "We really needed more flowers." Then, he leaned in to whisper in Daniel's ear. "You were my last hope for champagne or at least a box of chocolates."

"They're for the enjoyment of the one who did all the hard work." He winked at Deepa and then leaned in to kiss her on the cheek.

Sidd placed the flowers on the floor with others. The flat surfaces were full of gifts, and even more flowers. "Wait a minute! Last time I saw you, you were gimping around with a cane. Was that an act for sympathy?"

"No, no, craziest thing. I woke up this morning and my ankle felt great." As Daniel explained, a figure moved into the open doorway behind him. It was Melanie. She stood quietly and listened, arms crossed, lips pursed.

Oblivious to her, Daniel continued. "It's like a miracle. When I went to bed last night - I'm not kidding you - it was sore and swollen from being on it all day." Daniel was excited at the opportunity to reveal his inexplicable healing to his friends until he realized his audience was not hearing him. From Sidd's solemn demeanor he looked to Deepa, who seemed to be holding her breath. Both were focused behind him. Daniel slowly turned and finally saw his wife. An uncomfortable silence followed. Finally, Melanie moved, and, ignoring Daniel, stepped around him to kiss Deepa on the cheek and caress little Kamala. Daniel, now thoroughly deflated, stood helplessly and watched her.

The atmosphere in the room was frozen until Sidd drew Daniel aside, whispering again, "We should talk." Then he informed the women. "Daniel and I have some work to discuss. We'll go down to the lobby and let you gals chat in peace."

Sidd and Daniel walked down the corridor to the small empty lobby at the end, where they could talk alone. "Alright, what's the story with your ankle? Are you loaded up on Oxycontin? I mean, you should be limping a little."

"I don't really know what to think. I woke up this morning and it was fine."

Sidd regarded him skeptically. "Why am I feeling there's something you're not telling me?"

Daniel glanced around furtively before answering. "All right, full disclosure. I had something strange happen last night."

"Stranger than a miracle healing?"

"In a way, yeah. At about four this morning I wake up when something hits the house. I mean, hard and loud. I thought maybe it was a meteorite…or an asteroid. Pardon the hyperbole. I jump out of bed and run outside and there's nothing. But I see the most amazing sky overhead."

"It was overcast last night. All our roofs were closed."

"I know they were. That's what was so strange. There was just this opening in the cover, like a picture framed with clouds. Orion, Sirius, the Moon, they all had atmospheric halos, like Van Gogh had painted them. Oh yeah, and a huge white fireball flew slowly across the sky. But it was only for a few minutes. By the time I checked the side of the cabin it was ending."

"So, you were on…pot? LSD?

"No! I'm telling you that's just the way it happened. Sidd, it's like I was called outside to see it."

Sidd reacted in alarm. "By whom?"

Daniel only shrugged. Sidd considered this for a moment. "Does this have anything to do with your sudden interest in UFOs? You of all people taking a contactee like Adamski seriously. Yeah, I did my own research. The guy was a crackpot."

"I'm not so sure."

"You don't want to go there, Danny. And don't ever mention this lapse in judgment to anyone at work. *Der fuehrer* gets a hold of this, and your career could be toast…the pumpernickel kind. Now I'd better get back."

As they approached Deepa's room again, they saw Melanie's back receding down the hall; she was leaving. Daniel pulled Sidd back and whispered, "I want to catch Melanie. We need to discuss some things. Explain to Dee, will you?"

Daniel waved to Deepa from the doorway as he hurried past. He caught up as Melanie was just stepping into the empty elevator. When he moved in beside her, she did not acknowledge him.

On the ground floor the elevator door opened on the couple, still staring straight ahead, each aware of the other but not relating. As they stepped out to let those waiting in, Daniel finally reached out and grabbed Melanie by the arm to stop her. One hostile look from her and he quickly dropped his hold. "Sorry, but I really want to talk with you. Can we just sit here for a bit?"

Before them was the main lobby with a series of waiting sections framed by comfortable couches and easy chairs. They picked an unoccupied corner. Melanie clearly wanted to get it over with. "Okay, what?"

"Look, I know I screwed up. But we haven't slept together for six months."

"So that gives you the right to screw anyone you can? If we're going to feel sorry for ourselves, I've got a whole laundry list." She started to rise.

"No, no, wait…please"

Melanie settled back down but added, bitterly, "Well, she won't get pregnant. We know that's not gonna happen." When she saw how crushed Daniel was by her remark, she immediately regretted it. "I'm sorry I said that."

Daniel shrugged it off. "It's okay. I'm not making excuses. I did it. I was unfaithful. And I apologize for that. I never wanted you to find out because I knew it would hurt you."

"What's with you? Infidelity? That's not the man I know. And one day you're hobbling around injured and now you're fine."

"Some stuff is going on. I can't explain it myself. But I'd like to get things back to our new normal, if possible."

Melanie considered this while her eyes scrutinized him, then sighed. "I don't really care about your girlfriend. I was angry."

"Understood." He waved his hand in dismissal. "How's our boy doing?"

"He misses you. Doesn't know what is going on, obviously."

"How about I take him with me to the cabin for the weekend? He loves it up there. And I surely miss him."

Melanie pondered Daniel's request long and hard before her face finally softened and she nodded her assent. "I don't want to punish him." She was on the verge of saying 'or you' but couldn't quite get past her anger. "Okay. Pick him up Friday."

Melanie got up to leave. Daniel moved to embrace her, but she waved him off. They walked out together. At the valet stand he left her to wait for her car as he walked toward the parking structure where he picked up his Polestar. When he left the parking structure a black SUV with blacked out windows fell in a few cars behind him.

Chapter 8

Arriving at the Harbor House Restaurant on San Diego's waterfront, Daniel scanned the room until he spotted a distinguished man with a well-trimmed salt-and-pepper beard, Dr. Benjamin Bains, waving at him. He joined him at a table in a corner.

"Dr. Bains, I presume."

"In the flesh, Dr. James. But please, call me Ben. Thanks for taking this meeting, Daniel. I sensed a connection from our phone conversation."

"Got to admit I was intrigued by your credentials and background, Ben. Especially the film consulting. How'd you get into that?"

"There's a story there alright. Let's order and we'll get into it." He motioned a waiter over.

Later, their meals before them, they ate while they talked.

Dr. Bains was deep into his personal history. "Then I was a graduate student of Dr. Allen J. Hynek. Do you know who I'm talking about?"

Daniel shook his head.

"In the Sixties, Dr. Hynek was the foremost astronomer in the country, so the Air Force hired him to consult on Project Blue Book, their attempt to investigate UFOs. But

CHAPTER 8

its real mission was to discredit the whole subject of UFOs. They expected a man of Hynek's stellar reputation to join in their cover-up. But Dr. Hynek was a man of science and he realized UFOs deserved a real investigation. So, he took them seriously. When the Air Force officially shut down Blue Book, Dr. Hynek continued on his own and became one of the leading authorities on the subject in the world."

"But you've had this great career in gravitational research - the Einstein Medal? How did his rather eclectic career involve you?" Daniel leaned in across the table, interested in Bains' stellar accomplishments.

"We shared a common bonding experience, that was very… uncommon, you might say." Dr. Bains studied Daniel, gauging his reaction.

Daniel drew back and crossed his arms, not liking the direction the conversation was headed. He asked warily, "How so?"

"Unnatural activity by…craft."

"UFOs?"

"Extraterrestrial."

Bains' openness caught Daniel off guard. "How did you know that?"

"We were told."

"By whom?"

"Beings."

Daniel was uncomfortable now. His eyes swept the room furtively, to make sure no one was listening. Bains began to probe. "Have you ever seen anything unusual that you couldn't explain?"

Daniel squirmed in his seat and finally gave a barely perceptible nod.

"Recently?"

Daniel's guard went fully up. He refused to answer.

Bains assessed him and determined he had pushed enough. "Whatever you saw, Daniel, has probably convinced you that reality is not as science portrays it. Our government's contact with extraterrestrial civilizations - yes, it's real - and back-engineering of alien technology has existed for more than half a century. But...were this to be revealed prematurely, society would break down, religions would crumble overnight, anarchy would reign."

The fact that Daniel showed no surprise at Bains's sensational revelations convinced him that the young man had indeed made contact that night in the desert.

Daniel protested, "But science has a duty to truth."

"Some truths have to wait." Bains paused. When Daniel protested no more, he continued. "Daniel, my career turned out the way it did because I was given a choice and chose wisely. My advice is you tell no one about your recent experience and good things will come of it. You are now being watched by powerful people. People who hold the keys to your future." He waited to let his words sink in. "My organization is willing to offer you a position of importance...for your cooperation."

He pulled a business card out of his pocket and handed it to Daniel. Daniel looked it over carefully. "*Astralis* Academy?"

"We're the civilian organization behind the recent Air Force video disclosures."

"So, disclosure is happening?"

"All in good time...but only on our terms."

After mulling this over, Daniel finally spoke. "Ben, I don't remember speaking with you at the lecture. Someone of your stature and presence I think I would have remembered."

Dr. Bains just smiled noncommittally.

"You weren't there, were you?"

Now broadly grinning, Dr. Bains grabbed the check and rose while dropping a twenty on the table. "Lunch is on me. Think over carefully what I said. You'll be contacted sometime soon."

Daniel sat for a while staring out the window at the sun-sparkled harbor, deep in thought. If Bains was not at the lecture, then what was this all about? A ruse to get him here to be recruited by…whom? It also meant that Dr. Sauer had to be in on the plot. And it was clear Bains somehow knew that he had had a sighting at Joshua Tree. At last, he rose and exited onto the Embarcadero to walk and think things over.

On foot Daniel approached the corner of the busy intersection, where a mother and four-year-old boy were waiting for the light to change. The mother talked on her cellphone, distracted in conversation.

He had walked past when suddenly his face contorted as if he had just seen something horrifying. Immediately, he dashed back, snatched up the boy and ran toward the park, away from the corner.

The mother reacted instantly, screaming as she ran after him. "He's stealing my baby!"

This quickly drew the attention of other pedestrians in the park. Some came running after them.

As the mother and bystanders converged on him, Daniel stopped abruptly and handed the child to the mother. At that very moment from behind they heard a terrible screech of tires and a loud crash as an automobile plowed into the light pole where the two had been standing, driver slumped over and passed out.

The dumbfounded mother turned back from the scene in full awareness that Daniel had just saved their lives. She was too shocked to speak, but her eyes told it all. The crowd around the accident quickly grew and a bicycle beat cop arrived; in the confusion, Daniel slipped off unnoticed.

At a park bench away from the excitement, he sat down, buried his head in his shaking hands, and tried to fathom what had just happened. From across the park a man in a hoodie and dark sunglasses watched him, taping with his smart phone.

Daniel prepared for bed with a low-level trepidation of what might be coming. The incident on the Embarcadero had unnerved him. What had prompted him to grab that child? No internal voice had commanded him to do it. It was just a feeling, but he'd had such "feelings" all his life. What had made him act on this one, and so dramatically? And the repercussions if the accident had not occurred? He could have been arrested for kidnapping. He shuddered to think of it.

To add to his internal turmoil, all evening long he had heard strange noises in the cabin, noises that sounded like - yet he knew were not - normal house sounds. They'd been present since he moved into the cabin, but the frequency and intensity were elevated after the events of this extraordinary day. He'd been hearing them since that night in the desert when he saw what he saw…what he still hadn't been able to fully reconcile with his reality.

At first, he'd assumed the noises were natural. One in particular occurred whenever he sat in the easy chair in the living room. Since it seemed to emanate from the kitchen wall, he'd assumed it was caused by the pipes running through the wall, the natural expansion and contraction of metal with hot water flowing from the water heater. But then he noticed it occurred hours after he'd run water in the kitchen.

And in his bedroom at night. Whenever he awoke from sleep, he heard a pronounced snap in the room, as if something were announcing that he was alert and conscious. It was so regular that he started to think it was his imagination, as there was no logical, scientific reason he could fathom for the noise and its reliability. To settle the issue, one night he set up his video camera beside his bed to record his sleep. The next morning after a quiet night of no recalled noise, he reviewed the tape and realized 8 hours of listening to silence was no way to spend his Sunday, so he loaded the file into a video editing program he'd sometimes used to create YouTube videos. The program produced a visual graph of the audio tracks on his video files. As he scrolled through the file nothing unusual appeared. It was the most boring taping imaginable, hours of blackness with no sound. One consolation was he realized he did not snore. But as he zoomed in on one segment of the soundtrack something caught his eye, a little blip that could mean sound. He turned on the audio and there it was, the "snap," as clear as can be. In one sense he felt victorious, he was not imagining the sounds. But what was making them? As he scanned through the file again, listening whenever he saw the telltale blip in the graph, he realized the sound coordinated with his sleep pattern. Whenever he heard his breathing change and/or he stirred in bed, signaling he was about to awaken, he heard the loud snap. The conclusion was obvious: someone or something was monitoring his sleeping consciousness. Who…or what could it be? And why?

Pondering such incorporeal phenomena, trying to fit all the anomalies he was newly encountering into his new concept of reality occupied many of his waking hours now.

The rest of his free time away from work he spent reading books about UFOs, trying to decipher what other people's sightings might mean for what he, Byron and Hoshi had witnessed in the desert. But behind it always was a nagging feeling that there was more, much more than he could consciously recall. One of the books he'd read claimed that sinister government elements, the so-called black ops programs - Byron had said the helicopter was black ops military - that were unsanctioned by the normal government channels, were involved in highly classified research into psychic phenomena. One author even swore that these unacknowledged programs had developed electronic devices that simulated psychic abilities like telepathy and could interfere with people's thoughts, could even engineer dreams remotely. And there was more, some of a sinister nature. One prominent author in the field of ufology, a medical doctor, claimed that he and one of his key assistants had been sent, teleported via some Star Trek-like transporter it would seem, a rare form of cancer. His assistant had died of the disease and only by his enhanced psychic healing ability was the doctor able to combat the sustained attack.

Now there was the enigmatic Dr. Bains. Was the physicist part of this cabal of rogue government agents delving into such "dark arts"? Scientific officialdom scoffed at such psychic phenomena, refusing even to sanction experiments in subjects such as telepathy, though largely off-the-radar institutions like IONS, the Institute of Noetic Sciences, founded by former Apollo astronaut Dr. Edgar Mitchell, did conduct limited research in esoteric subjects.

With these bizarre new ideas spinning around in his mind,

CHAPTER 8

Daniel laid down and switched off the light. Almost immediately he heard a loud snap at the bedroom door. It was no normal settling sound, for it seemed to emanate from the atmosphere of the room, not the materials of the walls, or ceiling or floor. The room was abnormally quiet. He listened hard; there was no wind blowing in the pines outside. His senses went to ultra-high alert. Then he heard it again, an equally loud snap, only not quite in the same place. It had moved! And it was coming closer to him! Trying to suppress the rising panic of what that might mean, he silently said a prayer, rolled over, forced his eyes closed, and tried to sleep.

Amazingly, he dozed off rather quickly. At least he was surprised in retrospect, once he awoke and realized he'd been in a dream state. He had fallen almost immediately into a meditative state known to science as the "hypnagogic state" between wakefulness and sleep, when dreams are extremely vivid and real.

In his lucid dream he was walking along a path through natural dunes near an undeveloped seashore. But rather than enjoying a relaxing stroll in nature, he was tense, for he sensed someone was behind him, someone he knew, someone he did *not* trust. He abruptly stopped and spun around. There stood a man wearing a white cowboy hat. Immediately he recognized the man but could not put a name to him. As their eyes locked, Daniel knew he had caught the man by surprise, and the man was angry, seething with rage from the act of discovery. The sheer impetus of the man's glare shook Daniel out of his dream state, and he awoke.

As his eyes snapped open in the dark bedroom, he heard a loud, energy infused crack near the same place he had heard it prior to sleep. Only this time the energy had intensified and quickened with a sinister resolve. The source of the sound moved toward Daniel in the darkness; there could be no doubt. And he knew, just knew, that the energy behind that ominous crack was the rage and anger of the man in the white hat. And he was coming for Daniel.

Daniel said a small prayer. He was not an overly religious man, but at times in his life he had resorted to his childhood habit of praying for safety. Raised Protestant, he'd attended a small Baptist church with his family on holidays, but they were not regulars. His mother was certainly spiritual, though, and imbued him with the idea of a benevolent God that loved all souls regardless of whether they loved Him.

The source of the sound progressed, each succeeding crack in a little different position, a little closer, from the door across the foot of his bed, turned and came up the side, until it stopped beside him not 3 feet away. There were three loud pops the intensity of which he'd never experienced. He was under attack. Psychic attack! But there was nothing physical there!

He tried to focus his mind on God and loving thoughts but found it hard to concentrate. The entity was right beside him and seething with rage. He tried to meditate, sitting up in bed, in the dark, but his "monkey mind" was out of control, a panicked rhesus frantically fleeing through the jungle treetops.

Then something changed, the scientist awoke. He thought, real or product of my imagination, I must know what this is. He stopped praying, turned his torso to face the entity, and began conversing with it. Daniel talked about love and how God's unconditional love was available to all. He explained how he wanted to understand what was happening here, why the being was angry and threatening.

"I don't know who you are, and I don't know why this is

happening. But I want to understand. And if it's something I've done to you, I'm unaware of what it is. Please understand this and accept my apology."

Daniel felt liberated as he spilled his guts to a ghost. Voicing his feelings in the dark freed him to express even more; he began to purge himself of the doubts, inadequacies, shortcomings from his life. He said things that he had thought for years but never expressed to any living human being. And now here he was in the darkness of his bedroom expressing his deepest emotional desires, longings, fears to an unseen "sound", as if there were a living human being behind the energy he was feeling and hearing.

Then, amid all his venting and purging, something changed again, the entity behind the sound, now clearly right beside him, emitted a loud, audible "harrumph" that could only be interpreted as futility, a failure to accomplish whatever its dire intent had been.

And the entity diminished. Daniel felt it shrivel like a balloon with the helium leaking out. It did not leave but retreated into the corner near the bathroom door and waited there watching, listening, with perhaps a new respect for its "quarry." Daniel thanked it.

Uncommonly relieved, he felt the goosebumps, that had raked his skin since he'd first become aware of the entity, diminish. Daniel laid down and, suddenly aware of the chill in the air of the room, pulled the covers over his bare torso. Soon he was fast asleep, a peaceful dreamless sleep such as he had not had since before that night in the desert.

Chapter 9

The next morning Daniel, with his morning *LA Times* and a hot coffee in hand, settled into a seat at his regular coffee shop.

On the TV screen above a San Diego station news reader was reporting. "All of San Diego is abuzz with this feel-good story. A potentially fatal accident was averted yesterday, ironically at the corner known as Dead Man's Point, by a good Samaritan who then disappeared into the crowd."

On the screen now the young mother was being interviewed. "I thought he was kidnapping my baby, but he was actually saving our lives! Like our guardian angel."

Next up was a grainy indistinct video of a man sitting, head in hands, on a park bench. The news reader continued. "Is this the 'Angel of Dead Man's Point'? All of San Diego wants to know."

Daniel stared at the picture on the screen, then furtively buried his head in the paper.

In a comfortable development on the outskirts of Escondido, Daniel's Polestar sat in a driveway. Daniel opened the back door and Jesse jumped in. Melanie watched from the stoop and waved as they backed out to the street and drove away. Waiting down the block was the black SUV which followed

CHAPTER 9

Daniel at a discreet distance.

Daniel pulled into the driveway at the cabin and parked. He let Jesse out, who immediately dashed about the yard barking and chased a squirrel up a tree; at a safe height, the squirrel turned and barked back, scolding.

Through the trees, Daniel noticed the black SUV roll to a stop out on the main road. Wondering who it could be, he started walking down the driveway to get a better look. The vehicle immediately did a U-turn and drove back down the road.

Daniel emptied the contents of a can of dog food into a dog dish on the kitchen counter, sprinkled on a powder from a vitamin packet, then mixed it into the food before placing it on the floor, where Jesse greedily went to work on it.

"What a good boy you are, my love." Daniel patted Jesse on the head, who looked up quickly, to acknowledge the affection, while not interrupting the task at hand. He was a good boy, but it hadn't always been that way. As a puppy he grew fast and was ungainly around the house often imperiling the furniture and bare human legs as his tree switch of a tail whipped everything in its path. A veritable whirling dervish of energy Jesse's tail whipped cabinets, doors, tables, legs, like a water charged fire hose imperiling anything not nailed down. Luckily, California was earthquake country - though no one normally thought of it as lucky - and someone had invented two-sided tape and a sticky putty to secure valuables. So, while making their breakables Jesse safe, Daniel and Melanie also made them EQ safe.

When with another dog, Jesse's canine energy increased geometrically, especially when it was Sidd and Deepa's black lab, Jezebel, the same age as Jess and about the same size. Neither dog was disciplined and, when together, they whirled and jumped competing for attention. Although both were good-natured and playful, one couldn't stand to be around them for long. Slender Melanie simply could not handle them when she took the two for walks. Jezebel had stayed with them for two weeks one summer while Sidd and Deepa, long before sweet Kamala, traveled to India for a wedding. One day Melanie put them on separate leashes, one in each hand, and took them for a walk in the park. All was fine until competing doggy attractions took them in opposite directions. Too stubborn to let them go, Melanie was pulled along at their mercy and "wham" into a eucalyptus. There she stood straddling the tree, trunk against her nose as the two canine behemoths threatened to pull her apart, like some medieval torture rack. Luckily, neighbor kids saw her predicament and ran over to help. Melanie carried around a scab on her nose for a week or so as a reminder of the ordeal. When Daniel had mentioned she could have just let go, she responded, indignantly, that they were her responsibility, and neither were getting hit by a car on her watch.

Daniel had said, "You put me in mind of the monkey that won't let go of the large banana in a small necked jar."

To which Melanie rejoined, "I don't think that analogy fits, oh clever one."

"No, but the principles are the same."

When the traveling Sharmas returned the two dogs were immediately enrolled in obedience school and life became much less perilous in both households.

Daniel now turned to fixing his own supper and loudly shouted over his shoulder as he made for the refrigerator.

CHAPTER 9

"Alexa, music!"

Alexa gave her standard programmed response. "Here's a song I think you might like." Then out of the Echo wafted the mellifluous contralto of Karen Carpenter.

Daniel stepped into the living room with a Stouffer's Lasagna package still in his hand as his quizzical expression changed into a smile. The Echo continued to play the Carpenters' "Calling Occupants of Interplanetary Craft."

Daniel remembered the song from the Seventies and always thought it an odd choice for the straight-laced brother/sister duo. But now he marveled at how the lyrics openly referenced telepathy as a means of communicating with extraterrestrial beings, even calling for a World Contact Day.

While his meal baked, a quick online search revealed that the writers were not The Carpenters, but members of a group called Klaatu, named for the character in the Fifties science fiction flick *The Day the Earth Stood Still.* The song charted as a Top 40 hit in 1977 partly because of rumors Klaatu was really a secret reunion of the Beatles – it was not - and The Carpenters' cover. Daniel wondered: Was it just a gimmick song or were the authors and The Carpenters serious about its message?

Later that night Daniel lay in bed reading *The Day After Roswell* by retired Colonel Phillip Corso with Jesse bedded down at his feet. The title, of course, referred to the Roswell, New Mexico UFO case, the most famous UFO case in the United States.

The Roswell incident happened in the vicinity of an out-of-the-way air base in New Mexico just a few years after the cessation of hostilities in the Second World War.

In 1947, Roswell Army Air Field (RAAF) was the home of the

famous 509th Bomber Group which hosted the B-29 airplanes that bombed Hiroshima and Nagasaki and ended World War II. As such it was the only depository of the United States' nuclear bombs and therefore demanded the highest security in America's entire military environment.

Located just 5 miles North of the base, the city of Roswell experienced a boom during the War years, nearly doubling in population in the decade from 1940 - 1950 to around 26,000. It would be safe to say that Roswell was a military town, especially in 1947, a fact that was to have grave implications for the history of one of the most significant events of the 20th century or any century in the recorded annals of humankind.

It was hard to imagine now in the 21st century how different things were in the mid-20th, so much had changed in technology and communication; man had conquered space, at least over Earth, with the International Space Station and weather and communications satellites. But immediately following the war radar was a new technology and jet aircraft were largely in the testing stage, so the propeller planes that had won the war, the B-29s and P-51s, still ruled the skies. After a total War effort of combined civilian and military interests, a weary national citizenry enjoyed a collective sigh of relief, but the war machine could not afford such luxury given the continuous tensions with the Soviet Union.

Consequently, New Mexico in 1947, home of so much of America's cutting-edge technology, was quite possibly the most highly guarded area in the country and perhaps the entire world. There was Los Alamos, where the atom bomb was developed; White Sands, site of the captured German V2 rocket testing; the Trinity atom bomb test site was not far from Alamogordo, and Roswell was home to the 509th Bomb Group where the most famous bomber in the world, the *Enola Gay*, began her A-bomb mission that nearly obliterated Hiroshima.

Just a week before the events of July in Roswell (June 24, 1947, to be exact) another famous incident occurred that few at the time could have imagined would impact the world so dramatically. Civilian pilot Kenneth Arnold spotted 9 silver objects while on a flight over Washington State, describing them to the press as looking like saucers. Within days, headlines across the world were emblazoned with "Flying Saucers," and the UFO era was launched, though the actual acronym (for "unidentified flying object") was not coined till later with the Air Force's Project Blue Book. Though the image was new, the concept of extraterrestrial spaceships was not. The *War of the Worlds* radio broadcast of the HG Wells novel in October of 1938 had created a panic in parts of the country as the realism of the drama touched a fearful nerve in many listeners. Even the war years were not immune to reports of strange objects in the sky. The "foo fighters" were glowing orbs that numerous pilots reported following their planes over the skies of Europe and the Pacific. Arnold's sighting began a series of similar sightings across the US in the weeks and months to come and the American military took notice of this possible new threat to our sovereign airspace.

On the night of July 1, 1947, radar units across the state of New Mexico lit up with strange blips that streaked across their screens at phenomenal speeds. No one at the time knew what to make of it but all were seeing them: the Roswell 509th, White Sands guided-missile base, and the A-bomb testing facility at Alamogordo. Zipping across the screens with every sweep of the radar beacon at speeds impossible for any conventional technology, if they were aircraft, the UFOs operated with total impunity in the skies over New Mexico. Scrambled fighters, once in the sky, found nothing to report. If the cause of the radar returns were craft of unknown origin and design, then it was assumed they were from an enemy, possibly the Soviets, intent on learning the secrets of the top military technology of the age. Army Intelligence was put on high alert as the word went out to Washington of this potential threat to the security of the United States. Within hours, by order of the generals at the Pentagon, the best agents of the highly secret Army Counterintelligence service were dispatched to bolster the local units in Roswell, where they would infiltrate the civilian community to monitor any possible enemy activity.

Monsoon season in the environs of Southern New Mexico typically provided thunder and light storm extravaganzas that could last for hours, day or night. It was during one such violent display of nature's power that an extraordinary occurrence quite literally took the city and the world by storm. By various accounts on the evening of July 4, while most citizens, civilian and military, were celebrating our nation's costly victory in world conflict a scant 2 years before, radar operators at Roswell Air Field control tower were watching an unusual display of fireworks on their display screens. Multiple objects appeared to be making erratic flights around the area, sometimes increasing to speeds of over a thousand miles per hour, when suddenly one of the blips disappeared briefly, then reappeared as myriad white fluorescent dots on the radar screen only to blink out as if they had never existed. The consensus of all in the control tower radar room was that surely the craft, whatever it was, had crashed.

Believing the unidentified crashed object was an enemy craft that had been taking photographs of their top-secret military base, the radar officer immediately called the 509th Base commander, Col. William Blanchard with the news. "Bull" Blanchard at once authorized a retrieval mission to find the craft and secure the site to preserve the crashed vehicle for investigation and to safeguard the public from any unknown hazards. No one at the time knew what they would find but an aircraft that could maneuver right-hand turns at thousands of miles per hour was not powered by any conventional source. The nuclear age might have just begun, but the military was aware of the dangers of radiation fallout.

What happened next was the subject of controversy. The military team dispatched to find the object were not the only people at the scene: civilian campers hunting for Indian artifacts had witnessed the crash. But before making for the distant crash site, they radioed the news to the county Sheriff's office, who in turn notified the fire department to dispatch a pumper truck to the scene with a police escort.

When Col. Blanchard's 509th military team arrived, they immediately sealed the location to preserve it for the investigation to come. Their orders were to protect the site by any means necessary to prevent the dissemination of any information about it. At the center of the crash site was a curiously shaped craft with its nose embedded in the bank of an arroyo, its tail pointing skyward at 45-degrees. A squad of Military Police spread out to secure the area as other squads of soldiers began methodically gathering the crash debris.

But the curious craft was not the only odd thing about the crash site. There were the bodies. According to numerous witnesses in later years, including some of the key officers who were there, the ground was littered with bodies of small beings, hairless, child-sized gray-skinned beings with huge heads, some alive. These were loaded onto stretchers and into body bags and taken back to the base along with the nearly intact craft and the scattered debris. The delta-shaped flying "wing" about 30 feet long was hastily loaded aboard a flat-bed trailer, chained down and covered with a tarp, then driven, just after dawn, right through the main street of Roswell to the base south of town.

The retrieval operation was in full swing when the small convoy of civilian vehicles arrived. They were met at the perimeter and stopped by armed sentries. Before them they could see a large area of the desert lit up like a baseball field by a ring of floodlights with a scurry of activity on going beneath, and what looked like a wing shaped vehicle just being hoisted onto a flatbed trailer. In the confusion, one of the firemen was able to make his way beyond the perimeter to the crash site and even stood within a few feet of one of the stretchered bodies, still alive, as it was loaded into a truck. Soon after, he was discovered, questioned, and warned to leave the site and never tell anyone about what he had seen. He swore many years later, claiming the incident was seared into his memory like a brand, that the small being communicated its dying pain telepathically into his mind.

That night and in the days following military teams scoured the crash site covering every inch of ground for hundreds of yards around to sanitize it of any foreign material from the craft and occupants. On the base and in Roswell itself, a similar sanitizing of minds was taking place. Trained intelligence personnel warned civilians who were at the site or at the base at the time of the debris arrival, in the sternest and most intimidating manner. One woman who was only a young child at the time remembers a fierce helmeted Army rep yelling at her in the kitchen, while her parents cowered outside the door, that if she ever said anything to anyone about what her parents had told her, all of them would be taken out into the desert and never heard from again.

Yet despite these security efforts, Col. Blanchard, perhaps following his instincts to get such a monumental truth out to the public while lacking any specific orders to the contrary, authorized a news release by the base Public Relations Officer stating that the base had indeed recovered a downed space craft. This rightfully made front page headlines in the local paper and went out over the wire service to the world, creating an international sensation, only to be retracted a few days later as nothing more than a misidentified weather balloon. And thus, the legend of Roswell began.

What made the author Corso so compelling for Daniel was the man's credentials. They seemed impeccable, especially for someone writing about UFOs and alien beings, as Roswell was ufology's most famous (to some infamous) incident. In a long Army service career, Col. Corso had been the military "mayor" of Rome, after the Allied invasion in WWII, commanded NATO missile bases, and was President Dwight Eisenhower's daily intelligence briefer, while serving under Lt. General Arthur Trudeau of Korean War fame (Battle of Pork Chop Hill). Corso himself was not at Roswell but did see one of the alien bodies when they were being transported across country by truck and stopped off for a night at his duty station in Fort Riley, Kansas.

Daniel was reading Corso's account when, suddenly, it hit him. "This is real." It was an epiphany to which his whole body reacted with a shuddering chill. He knew on a cellular level that it was true. And he admitted it frightened him to think that there were beings that looked the way Greys were often described and had the power to communicate through thoughts and that could, via various abduction scenarios, come in the night and take you away to a spacecraft flying high above the earth and do experiments on you…and you had no control over it. What a disturbing thought. How many times had he glibly dismissed his audience's questions about Roswell, as he had done during his last lecture? Believing and espousing the "party line" of the military, he had never really considered that they might be covering up the truth, until now. Daniel let the book fall on his chest. "Roswell really happened!"

Jesse suddenly growled; his attention fixed intently at the corner of the room near the master bathroom door.

"What's the matter, boy?"

Jesse barked, his gaze not wavering from the corner.

"It's alright, Jesse."

But just then a loud crack emanated from the corner. "What the hell!?" Daniel jumped out of bed to check out the corner but could find nothing wrong. "Sounded like the wall split." Remembering the entity in the white hat, he addressed the corner. "Is that you? What kind of games are you playing here? You need to stop it. I'll not be intimidated by you!"

He climbed back in bed as Jesse nuzzled in for comforting.

"Jess, my boy, thank goodness you aren't judgmental. I'm really not going crazy, though any human would probably think so."

He turned out the light then rolled over and draped his arm over Jesse beside him. In the dark as Daniel dropped off, Jesse continued staring at the corner.

CHAPTER 9

The digital clock on the nightstand read 2:30 when Daniel awakened. He rose to use the bathroom then settled back in beside Jesse. As he relaxed completely, drifting off, a marvelously pure musical tone filled his mind. The tone seemed to emanate from nowhere in particular and everywhere at once, a pure sound from no instrument he had ever heard. He felt a brief surge of motion and then he was free, floating. Daniel's ghostly astral body, a transparent image of himself, rose from his sleeping physical body to stand beside the bed in the cabin, lit in an eerie astral twilight. Jesse was awake, highly alert and seemed to sense Daniel's astral presence, perhaps even saw him. Astral Daniel continued to rise through the roof, oblivious to gravity or physical matter, and was suddenly free floating above the cabin in the clear night air. Euphoric to be flying, really flying, he rose higher and higher looking down on the forested mountains under the ghostly light of the quarter moon. Feeling the cool breeze on his skin - his astral body sensations seemed the same as on his physical body - invigorated him. He rolled, tumbled, rocketed up and dived down, skimming the treetops. On impulse he made for the moon - nothing seemed impossible - only to stop himself at what seemed thousands of feet high to marvel at the mountain landscape below him, the hilltops increasingly shrouded in mist as they retreated to the horizon; the trees and outcroppings of rock shimmered in the pale moonlight.

Off in the distance shone the city lights of Escondido and he thought, "Melanie." Suddenly he was over the city, looking down on their house. He thought of her in bed, and in an instant he had dropped through the roof and was standing in their bedroom gazing at his peacefully sleeping wife. As he watched her lovingly, longingly, she reached out in sleep to grab the pillow next to her and cuddle it as if she sensed his presence…and missed him, in the flesh, beside her. Daniel floated around to the other side, ready to climb in next to her, when two arms reached out from the shadows and grabbed him by the shoulders.

Suddenly back in his body, Daniel cried out, kicking violently, and woke himself up. He sat on the edge of the bed pondering the dream as Jesse licked and nuzzled his cheek comfortingly. "Oh, Jess. What's happening to me? These strange fantastical dreams. What can I trust is reality anymore?"

He lay back down. Jesse nestled on Daniel's chest, gazing up at him, as Daniel gently stroked his head and ears.

"If I could time travel, boy, I'd go back to happier times… when she was my angel." His mind drifted off.

Daniel was just walking into the Reiki Angels shop. In the quiet and dim waiting area, lit by scented candles with soft meditative music playing, Daniel approached the seated receptionist, Iris, who was staring intently at her computer screen. Without looking up she addressed him. "Who are you here to see?"

"Melanie."

"Do you have an appointment?"

"Yes."

Finally, Iris looked up. "Oh. Daniel. Nice to see you again. Mel is with a client right now but she is expecting you. Please have a seat."

Daniel took a seat along the wall with a view down the hall to the treatment rooms. In a few moments a door opened, and a handsome young man came out, followed by Melanie. They

CHAPTER 9

moved to hug, but she stopped him, altering the embrace to the opposite side. "Remember? Heart chakra to heart chakra."

As he watched them warmly hugging, Daniel found himself jealous. The young man departed, and Mel turned her attention to him. "Daniel, come on back."

He entered the room behind Melanie, who closed the door. One candle lit the room and a stick of incense burned in a stand next to it. "Now you said you'd never done Reiki before, right?"

"First time."

"Wonderful, you're in for such a treat. Please remove your shoes and lie on the table face up."

Once he was positioned Mel turned on the music. The ethereal sounds of "Angel Love" by Aeoliah wafted from the built-in ceiling speakers. Melanie explained the process. "Reiki works with the flow of the chi through the energy meridians of the body. I'll be opening and clearing your chakras today. All you do is lay still as I pass my hands over you. I'll not actually be touching you at any time, but you should feel the energy flowing from my hands. If you feel anything opening just try to let it go without resistance. Ready?"

He nodded and concentrated on calming his racing mind, intent on pleasing her. She began at the head (crown) chakra and slowly worked her way down, leaving her hands hovering over each chakra for several minutes before moving on to the next. Daniel closed his eyes and relaxed. As Melanie reached the 4th chakra, over the heart, she maneuvered her hands in a spiral motion up and away. Suddenly Daniel began to feel overpowering emotion. He softly wept and could not stop. Melanie quietly left the room to allow Daniel privacy. When she reentered Daniel was sitting up on the side of the table.

"I'm sorry. I don't know what came over me."

"What you had was a perfectly normal reaction to the release of pent-up energy. Not many people, especially men, can achieve that on the first treatment. It's a good sign that your whole body wants to heal."

"And that I have a good healer."

Melanie smiled reassuringly. "That's all for today. We always close with a hug."

As Daniel stood, before she could instruct him, he said, "Heart to heart."

Melanie smiled at his precociousness, and they embraced warmly, an embrace that went on for longer than a formality, a hug at once very personal and that foretold of good things to come.

In Daniel's mind, the scene morphed into a romantic setting, their entwined figures in the sunset on a Pacific beach, where the embrace had now become a long passionate kiss.

Daniel was now peacefully sleeping, arms wrapped around Jesse nuzzled in beside him.

Chapter 10

At his regular coffee shop Daniel sat down with his coffee and paper next to a young man working from his laptop. When the man went for a coffee refill, Daniel noticed the screen displayed a Big Blue Marble shot of Earth with the overlay "Are You Ready to Make Contact?" When the man returned, he inquired about it. "That's a provocative question. Does it mean what I think it means?"

"Oh yeah, it's advertising a new UFO convention in the desert. All the ufology big shots will be there. If you're interested, check out their website: 'Contact in the Desert.'"

Daniel did just that. Contact in the Desert, it seemed, was a new convention convening in the desert this summer themed on all things UFO and alien: abductions, crop circles, time travel, cattle mutilations, etc. Some of the presenter names Daniel recognized from his ufology research: a noted radio host of a late-night program on the bizarre, the great granddaughter of a US President, an ex-lumberjack whose experience with a UFO had been made into a Hollywood film, a doctor who specialized in alien implant removal.

One name intrigued him, Maxine Braun, a hypnotherapist from California that specialized in alien abductee regression and would be doing a group hypnosis demonstration. Might she be the key to unlocking the hidden memory of that night in Joshua Tree?

Back in the data room Daniel was again on his computer as Sidd came in behind him. He noticed the 'Contact in the Desert' website screen.

"Buddy, more ETs? When does it end?"

"I think I'll go to this UFO convention at Joshua Tree on Saturday. It could be fun. Interested?"

"Damn, you're incorrigible. No, Deepa wants to go to San Diego. Stroll the harbor front with our sweet little Kamala." He leaned over and whispered, hand covering his mouth in mock confidence. "I think she secretly wants to see where the Miracle of Dead Man's Point happened."

"What?"

"Haven't you heard? The Angel of Dead Man's Point is the talk of San Diego."

"Oh… Yeah."

"Personally, I think it was a kidnapping gone wrong, and the guy got lucky. Except the guy was white. Hell, from the description, it could be anyone. Even you."

As Sidd walked away, Daniel suppressed an urge to just blurt out "It was!" But he feared releasing a can full of slick and slithery truths, that would, like worms, be hard, if not impossible, to contain again.

Pickleball was a fast-growing racket sport, a hybrid between ping pong and tennis. Easy to learn and play for young and old alike without a long learning period like tennis. Brandishing a squarish wooden racket larger than a ping pong paddle, one hit a specially sized wiffle ball back and forth over a low net on a court roughly one third the size of a tennis court.

Sidd and Daniel were playing a game of singles pickleball at the Castle Creek Pickleball Courts. Ahead late in the set, Sidd was going for the kill when he inadvertently stepped into the "kitchen," a neutral zone on each side of the net, where a player may not stand while hitting the ball. The serve then passed to Daniel, who quickly won the next three points versus a deflated Sidd. Game, set, match. They exited, grabbed a cold bottle of water each from an ice chest for members and settled on a bench in the shade to cool off.

"Still going to San Diego tomorrow?" Daniel asked.

Reclined with eyes closed, Sidd nodded while fanning himself with his racket.

Daniel had been thinking about this moment ever since that day on the Embarcadero. He had to confide in someone. The secrets were piling up inside him to a pressure point, where he feared one might spill out inadvertently, causing an avalanche of veracity that could damage his career and relationships irreparably. Like a hot water heater, he needed to vent excess pressure. Melanie had been his pop-off valve, his best friend as well as wife, but was no longer an option. Sidd was the logical next choice. He began cautiously. "Buddy, there's something I need to tell you."

A few moments later, Sidd was sitting up straight, fully alert, intently staring at Daniel who had just finished his disclosure. After a long pause, he spoke.

"You're the fucking ANGEL OF DEAD MAN'S POINT?"

Daniel was visibly relieved. "I was afraid you wouldn't believe me."

"Who would make that up!?" Sidd screamed, then lowered his voice mid-sentence as he realized those playing on the court might hear him.

"Yeah. But, man, you can't tell anyone." Daniel implored him.

"Who would believe me?"

Sidd's illogic somehow made perfect sense given the circumstances and Daniel felt licensed to elaborate. "I'm changing, Sidd, and it scares me. I've been having these strange out of body experiences for a while. But this is the first time I've had a vision of something before it happened."

Staring at Daniel with real concern, Sidd tried to understand the bizarre confessions spilling out of his friend. "Precognition. You see the future?"

"I guess."

"Does this have anything to do with that desert hike?" Sidd asked, as if he already knew what the answer would be.

A few moments later, following Daniel's second revelation, Sidd wore an even more exaggerated look of astonishment.

"You saw a FUCKING MOTHER SHIP?" he screamed again. This time Daniel motioned for him to quiet down.

Sidd suddenly jumped up and paced in agitation.

"Yeah, and the next morning we were buzzed by this black military-like helicopter."

"Man, enough!" He waved his hands before Daniel's face, as if to cancel out any further talk on the matter. "Danny, I love you like a brother, but this is hard to take in. From normal guy to superhero and fucking alien - what? - Ambassador - in one sitting. I gotta think…." He started off toward the parking lot.

"Buddy, please don't tell anyone," Daniel pleaded.

"I'll…I'll call you later."

As his closest friend hurried to distance himself from him, Daniel leaned back and let out his own scream of frustration.

Chapter 11

On the campus of the Institute of Mentalphysics in Joshua Tree, California, a high desert complex designed by Frank Lloyd Wright Jr., Daniel, wearing his Pantropic fedora and dark sunglasses, strolled among the myriad vendors of ufology, the paranormal, New Age services and paraphernalia at the first Contact in the Desert convention.

As he walked about the dusty sand paths in the rustic setting, he dialed up a call to Sidd on his cellphone and was frustrated once again when it went right to voicemail; still he left another message. "Hey, buddy, it's me again. Please give me a call."

At a flowing water fountain near the center of the grounds he spied an empty bench and sat down to leaf through a small slickly printed pamphlet that contained the speakers' schedules. From a map at the center of the document Daniel traced his route to the proper venue.

In the modest building of about 300 capacity, Daniel sat down and read the blurb on the subject, alien abduction, and then a short bio of the lecturer, hypnotherapist Maxine Braun, who'd written several books on the subject.

Braun, a small, dark-haired woman in her Fifties, now stood before a packed crowd. It was hot in the building and people were fanning themselves and sweating profusely, but no one left. Daniel sat toward the back, observing with great interest as Maxine presented her theory of hypnotic regression.

"In my thirty years of administering to victims of alien abductions I've concluded that they suffer from PTSD much like any war veteran. The night terrors, flashbacks, shadow people, unexplained bouts of crying - the symptoms are all there. Many go undiagnosed for years, perhaps their whole lifetime. Through hypnotic regression they can regain lost memories of these traumatic events with the proven techniques of pioneers like Bud Hopkins and John Mack. Brought to the light of day these traumas can then be healed. Perhaps you are suffering from all or any of these symptoms, or just know there is something important in your life you can't remember. Or you get flashback images of events that you consciously think never happened. Hypnotherapy could help you to recall these events."

On the large LED screens to either side of Maxine were pictures of Dr. John E. Mack's book *Abduction: Human Encounters with Aliens*. Daniel wrote down the title in a small notebook.

Maxine continued. "Today we're going to try a group regression. Anyone here who feels uncomfortable can leave the room for this or just not follow the suggestions I'll give to induce trance."

Daniel stayed and even tried to take the suggestion.

Maxine's voice was soft and soothing. "Close your eyes, relax, breathe in, hold, now breathe out slowly."

Daniel face was relaxed, his eyes closed, and he was breathing gently.

"Breathe in, hold, breathe out. Let your mind go back in time and place to that moment you want to recall."

CHAPTER 11

In Daniel's mind he was back in the desert on the night of his sighting. He saw the mother ship rise from behind the mountain and tilt toward him until it was directly overhead. Then suddenly before him only inches away from his face, flashed the image of an alien face with two giant, slanted, black, teardrop-like eyes. Daniel was abruptly jolted out of his trance.

"Five, four, three, two, one. Awake. You are now completely in the present." As Maxine was bringing the group out of the trance, Daniel pondered the image that had flashed before him in meditation. The short group regression ended; Maxine opened the floor for questions and opportunities for audience members to relate their experiences. "Would anyone like to share a recall experience?"

A woman in the section to the left of Daniel rose and Maxine acknowledged her.

"Yes, my name is Claire. I remembered being on a ship with all these children around me. This tall alien being was telling me they were my children. And they needed my love and attention, something they, the aliens, could not give them."

"That's not an uncommon, repressed memory. Tell me, do you have children?"

"I have three. But I've also had a strange miscarriage."

"Go on. If you feel comfortable telling us. Was there a fetus?"

"Two. I was having twins, at least up until the beginning of the second trimester. That's what was so strange, one of the fetuses just disappeared as if it had been taken out of my womb. The doctors said it had been absorbed by the uterus but is that even possible?"

"I've had other clients tell me the same thing. The conclusion seems to be that the aliens were using you as a surrogate womb until the fetus was developed enough so they could care for the child themselves. Claire, thank you for your courage in sharing your experience with us."

When the lecture was over, Daniel hung around on stage as the crowd of people talking and getting books signed by Maxine dwindled. When the last person stepped away and Maxine was free, he stepped forward. "Ms. Braun, are you taking new clients?"

"Oh yes, I always try to save time for new clients. Are you interested yourself?"

"Possibly. Is it strictly private? Does therapist/patient confidentiality apply?"

"Yes, of course. What is your name?"

Daniel hesitated momentarily but decided he could be forthcoming with Maxine, who radiated warmth and trust. "Dan. But I have to be very discreet, as my professional life would suffer if it ever became known I was seeing someone like you." Realizing he might have just insulted her, he apologized. "I didn't mean that the way it came out."

Maxine was unfazed. "Don't worry. I understand very well. Many of my clients are professionals and were cautious at first. Do you mind telling me, in general, what you do?"

"I'm a scientist…an astronomer."

"Then I more than understand. Your colleagues probably put down the whole UFO phenomenon as craziness. Well, Dan, let me give you my card. If you decide to do the preliminary interview, call me and we'll set it up. We'll talk in general and then decide if treatment is something you want to try."

She handed Daniel her business card. He stepped away and then turned back and said gravely, "I saw something that shouldn't have been, not in the world I thought I knew."

CHAPTER 11

"One thing you will learn, Dan, is that you are not alone. In every sense of the word."

As Daniel exited the building, he was stopped by a man wearing a Hawaiian shirt, dark sunglasses, and a straw sun hat. "I know you, don't I?"

"No, I don't believe so." Daniel hurriedly moved away from the man and into the crowd flowing to other venues. The man gazed after him, intently.

On a sand path behind the Retreat Center complex Daniel walked alone toward the parking lot. He rounded a corner into a secluded portion of the walkway. There he met an attractive young woman walking quickly toward him. She was very exotic looking with short hair and a slim figure, clad in tank top and leotards, with large eyes that swept dramatically upward. She smiled sweetly as she passed by and gently touched him on the left shoulder. He thought he heard a soft feminine voice say, "Hello, dear."

Daniel was confused by such a term of endearment from a stranger. He walked on a few steps then halted abruptly. "Her lips didn't move!" he muttered to himself. Daniel swiftly pivoted to hail the woman, but she was not in sight. He sprinted after her. Rounding the corner, he saw the pathway beyond was empty except for an older couple coming toward him. He accosted them, breathing hard from the physical exertion. "Which way did that young woman go?"

Befuddled by the question, the elderly man asked, "What woman?"

"The one that just went by here!" Daniel shouted, impatiently.

"We haven't seen anyone on this path but you."

"But…." Daniel paled as if he had seen a ghost. Perhaps he had.

Concerned, the elderly woman placed a gentle hand on his shoulder. "Are you okay, dear?"

Chapter 12

Sidd was already at his desk when Daniel arrived on Monday morning. Daniel slammed his briefcase down. "Glad to see you're alive and well!" he said, wondering if Sidd picked up on his sarcasm.

The noise startled Sidd, but he remained cool. "Why wouldn't I be, buddy?"

"Didn't you get my messages?"

"Sure."

"And you didn't think to respond?"

"I knew I'd see you at work."

Daniel walked over to stand behind Sidd so he could whisper. "Are we gonna ignore the two-ton elephant in the room?"

"What do you mean?"

"I mean our pickleball conversation!" Daniel shouted.

"Oh, that. I've got too much on my plate to get involved with your dramas."

"My dramas?"

"Yeah. Now if you don't mind, Dr. Sauer wants my project outline today," he said, then added nonchalantly, "He said I have a good shot at promotion when he retires."

Daniel finally took his seat, amazed at Sidd's denial.

Daniel reposed on a recliner with Maxine behind him. He had just finished a hypnotherapy session and was fully alert but obviously dejected. "Don't feel like you've failed, Daniel," Maxine consoled him. "It can take time for the unconscious to open. Some of my clients have resisted hypnosis for months until they could finally relax enough to go into trance. But remember, a breakthrough can come at any time."

Daniel was not reassured. "I just have this nagging feeling something is there, but I can't grasp it."

"Do you meditate?"

"I used to regularly but haven't for years."

"You might consider trying it again. It could help you to relax in session."

"I can do that," he said, then began wringing his hands.

"Is there something else?"

He hesitated, ill at ease, then took a deep breath. "Maxine, I'm changing in ways I don't understand."

"Go on, Daniel. What you say here is confidential." She reached over and switched off the recorder she used for hypnosis sessions.

This relaxed him some, and he went on, "I've gotten so psychic; I sometimes know things before they happen. How is that possible?"

"Precognition is real. Though I'm sure it's hard for the scientist in you to accept."

Daniel's expression said, 'Tell me about it.' "And I had this really vivid flying dream."

"That could be an OBE. Out-of-body experience. Are you familiar with astral projection?"

Daniel nodded cautiously. "Leaving the body? I've read about it; it sounds like pseudoscience."

"You might be surprised how some reputable scientists view the topic. I suggest you look at the Monroe Institute and books by Robert Monroe. Monroe was a pioneer in the field and developed a sound wave technique that aids the brain in meditation and can even facilitate OBEs."

Daniel was skeptical but curious. His dream of flying in the night sky over the cabin and their home in Escondido was not a normal dream, he knew that. He was searching for answers and could not leave any stone unturned. Could he have left his body? But that begged the question of *what* left his body? Dangerous ground for a rational man of science.

Maxine went on. "Daniel, with alien contact comes the paranormal - psychic powers, even ghosts. It's a given in this business. Those flying dreams might be good signs that you are close to a breakthrough."

A breakthrough to what? Daniel asked himself. Maxine wasn't saying it, but she was thinking what he'd been suspecting, and feared to give voice to.

"You think I was abducted that night," Daniel said matter-of-factly. He turned round to look her in the eyes.

Maxine kept a poker face; she was trained not to influence a client with her own views. "We'll get to the bottom of it."

Daniel didn't press the issue.

Maxine continued. "You know, it might help you to talk with other experiencers. Abductees. Though I don't like that term for my clients. Abduction connotes negativity and some of these experiences are positive. Shortly after starting my practice, I formed a group of clients and former clients for this purpose. A group place to listen and share in a judgment-free environment. If you feel comfortable doing so you can attend a meeting and hear what others have to say about their experiences. You can share or not depending on how you feel. You don't even have to divulge your identity if you don't want to.

Daniel was immediately defensive. "Go public? I can't."

"We have a small group of people from all over the Southwest. Chances of meeting someone who knows you are slim. My suggestion would be to come once as my guest and just listen."

"I'll have to think about it."

"Fair enough. Let me give you the particulars."

Maxine wrote the info on a business card and handed it to Daniel.

Daniel meditated on the bedroom floor of the cabin sitting lotus style, legs crossed, hands resting on his knees, palms up. Though not as limber as he had been years ago when he had practiced transcendental meditation at an ashram in Long Beach, with a little stretching he was able to assume the position in reasonable comfort. A single candle burned before him as white smoke wafted from a small incense burner. The Echo played sitar meditation music.

After only 20 minutes of breathing and relaxation techniques, his mind was in a good place. There was a tug at his torso, like discarnate arms were pulling him up and his astral body rolled over and was out, free. It was all so natural that he thought nothing of it. His astral body continued rising to the ceiling, then turned to look down upon his physical body. From the couch Jesse stared up at him. On seeing his meditating form below, he thought, that's me! Immediately Daniel snapped back into his body. His awakened face registered his shock, then smiled in satisfaction acknowledging his first self-generated out-of-body (OBE) experience. Jesse came over from the couch to nuzzle him affectionately. Daniel kissed him on the head. "I love you, Jesse." He rose and immediately went online to look up the Monroe Institute.

Maxine had been right. There was much more written on OBEs and astral projection than Daniel had imagined. In the 1950's, Robert Monroe had been a successful radio producer in New York that had used his company to research the effects of sound patterns on consciousness. Using himself as a test subject for these audio experiments, he began having episodes that were called "out-of-body experiences". So impressed was he by these events that he devoted the next 20 years of his life to exploring the phenomenon and wrote several personal experience books on the subject including the groundbreaking *Journeys Out of Body*.

But Monroe was not a trained scientist, so Daniel pressed on in his research. Another book *Demystifying the Out of Body Experience* by Luis Minero treated the subject scientifically with a complex terminology. It was included in a branch of science not quite in the mainstream called conscientiology or the study of consciousness in all forms including multidimensional. The International Academy of Consciousness described it thus: "Conscientiology differs from conventional sciences in that its scientific foundation is based on a new, more advanced philosophical paradigm. Whereas conventional sciences are based on the Newtonian-Cartesian model, which considers reality to be unidimensional (physical only), conscientiology is based on the consciential paradigm, which considers reality to be multidimensional."

It was shocking to discover that some scientists were indeed taking a formerly taboo subject seriously, waking up to the reality that consciousness was part of the material world around us and could not be dismissed as a "brain phenomenon" outside of the purview of scientific method. As an astronomer/physicist, Daniel knew of the Copenhagen interpretation of the uncertainty principle in quantum physics, that the character of an electron as particle or wave was determined by the consciousness of the experimenter, and therefore, consciousness itself was fundamental to reality. If the mind affected the very nature of the energy that made up elementary particles, in a sense created the world, could mind or consciousness also create other worlds, worlds that existed in other dimensions?

He could not forget his own recent experience at Joshua Tree. The mother ship had just disappeared, winked out as the F-18s approached; Byron had said it slipped into another dimension. How could he disbelieve his own eyes along with two corroborating witnesses? This and his consciousness-expanding astral traveling on a parallel plane of existence, conspired to open Daniel up to this possibility. How could he deny it? Reality *was* multidimensional.

And the astral plane was one of those dimensions. Proponents claimed we all disconnected from our bodies each night in sleep, the majority just don't remember. Some sensitives had even observed the astral body suspended a few inches above sleeping people. Astral travel was claimed to be a learnable skill, though some individuals came about it naturally; the ability could be learned and controlled. So many experiential books had been written on the subject, that one could not dismiss the authors' similar experiences as anomalies.

Then there was remote viewing, which seemed to be a variant of astral projection whereas the mind only moved beyond the body into space to gain unquestioned information

CHAPTER 12

in controlled experiments. Somehow the mind and astral body could act like separate entities but were entwined, parts of a whole that need not share the same experience. One felt the astral body in astral travel, but in remote viewing, which only involved consciousness, did not. It was well documented that the CIA and the Soviet KGB had used remote viewing to spy on each other with apparent success. Ingo Swann and Joseph McMoneagle, the most famous remote viewers, had written multiple books on the subject.

The evidence was accumulating, including data, scientific-method-derived data in reputable peer-reviewed publications that Daniel could not dismiss. All in all, testimonials, scientific evidence, and not least of all, his own personal experience, convinced Daniel astral travel was real. He decided he must develop this skill.

In a private meeting room of a large hotel chain, the monthly gathering of Experiencers Together (ET) was in progress. Fifteen people, men and women of all ages, were seated in a u-shaped arrangement around tables with Maxine presiding at the head table. Patrick, a brash young man in his mid-twenties, had the floor, though he remained seated while animatedly relating his latest experience; "So, I took a swing at the little Grey bastard…"

At that moment, to Maxine's surprise, Daniel walked in. She interrupted, "Excuse me for one moment, Patrick. Group, I want you to all meet a guest of mine, Daniel."

The group collectively greeted him, to Patrick's great annoyance; He liked to be the center of attention.

"Daniel, I'm so glad you could make it. Have a seat anywhere."

Daniel sat at the far end of the table arrangement and quietly settled in to listen.

Another member Dallas, a middle-aged woman, spoke next before Patrick could continue. "I think it's so cool that Patrick actually took a swing at a Grey alien. A lot of us would like to do that."

"Oh yeah," Patrick went on. "The leader took me serious after that. And he tells me that I've been part of their breeding program for a long time."

Another woman, Claire, interjected a thought. "You look familiar to me. Do you think we could be part of the same program?"

Observing all with great interest, Daniel perked up as he recognized Claire from Maxine's group hypnosis session at the Contact in the Desert convention.

Patrick appeared flattered at some apparent implication that Daniel did not understand. But for the most part he was discounting Patrick's tale as likely exaggerated from the young man's braggadocio.

"Maybe," said Patrick. "Are your aliens from Zeta Reticuli?"

"They've mentioned Orion."

"Those groups are rivals, I think. So I doubt if we've been together."

Maxine, seeing how the conversation was bogging down into an exchange that could be handled person to person, took control. "You two can discuss that privately after we adjourn. Does anyone else want to share? Daniel? You are welcome to join in but as it's your first time it's certainly okay to just listen. There's never any pressure on any of us to contribute."

Daniel shook his head 'no' but then immediately reconsidered. "Wait! There is something that happened recently that has me baffled. I was at Contact in the Desert and a very exotic young woman acted as if she knew me, but I'd never seen her before. She walked by and tapped me on the shoulder and said, 'Hello, dear.'"

Patrick quickly added. "And her lips never moved, did they?"

Surprised at how Patrick had anticipated his issue with the event, Daniel turned his full attention to the young man. "No, I don't think they did."

"That's happened to me a lot. There's this one woman, older, who I've seen maybe a dozen times over my life. She always looks right at me and I hear her in my head."

Daniel didn't quite know what to make of Patrick's quick and incisive assessment of the encounter. It was almost like the young man was in Daniel's head. Or was it just a tactic to manipulate attention back onto himself, where he obviously liked it? Regardless, Daniel now had new respect for the young man and wanted more information. But before he could question him further, Patrick was on to another personal tale of his alien prowess. Daniel would have to follow-up with him later.

When the meeting was over, as people milled about chatting in small groups, Daniel approached Patrick. "Did you ever find out who this woman was?"

"Not exactly. She seems to be some sort of messenger. But I think she also might have been one of my partners."

"Partners?"

Patrick made a crude gesture with his hands, inserting his right index finger into a hole made by his left index finger and thumb.

"Sexual?" Daniel could not hide his shock at the young man's implication.

Amused at Daniel's prudishness, Patrick asked, "You surprised? That's what this abduction is all about, creating hybrid babies. The young woman you saw might have been a partner of yours…or your kid."

"My child?"

"Yeah. You married? Have kids?"

"Yes, and no, we don't have any children."

"That you know of." Patrick winked knowingly, then drifted off to where Claire was talking with Maxine, leaving Daniel to consider a new twist in his quest for the truth. An older man, Peter, who had been observing the two from nearby, now approached Daniel.

"Well, first timer, learn anything?"

"Maybe more than I wanted," Daniel answered dryly.

Peter laughed. "This business can have that effect on a newbie." He offered his hand. "Peter."

Shaking his hand, Daniel quipped. "So, Peter, how many hybrid kids do you have?"

This elicited a belly laugh. "Yeah, I heard that. It's not all about breeding." Then he leaned in close. "For someone as young as Patrick - all those raging hormones…" He winked. "I can see how he could think that. And perhaps it is all about mating…for him. But I doubt if ET would want DNA from an old fart like me."

He became very serious. "For me there is a big spiritual component."

"Are you religious?"

"Hardly, I was an atheist until I got into this stuff. Now I don't know what I am. I just know I believe in a higher power than man."

"How did you get into it?"

"I was in the Air Force stationed at Nellis AFB when I was

'volunteered.'" He air-quoted. "Special duty out at Groom Lake. You know, Area 51. The PTSD started after that. I'd get flash memories of things that never happened but seemed so real and stuck with me. For years I struggled about what to do until Maxine regressed me and it all started to make sense. How 'bout you?"

"I had an…incident out in the desert that I'm trying to figure out."

"Missing time?"

Daniel shrugged; he was getting uncomfortable.

Noting his reticence Peter did not press the issue. "Well, stick with it, is all the advice I have. Maxine will get amazing stuff out of you."

Chapter 13

Daniel sat down to enjoy his meal, Thai takeout he picked up on his way home from the ET meeting. Before him were arrayed paper cartons and Styrofoam containers of his favorites, Spring rolls, Tom Kha Kai, the spicey coconut milk soup, and Pad Thai noodles with pork. He'd ordered the same as he had for he and Melanie, anticipating there would be plenty of leftovers tomorrow night thus saving him one more meal to prepare. He was feeling good about himself after talking with Maxine's group. What Maxine had said was true - it was good to know there were others who shared similar experiences, the isolation was less debilitating when knowing others had gone through the doubt and fear you were experiencing. He looked to his Echo with a devilish gleam. "Alexa, what surprise you got for me tonight, babe?"

"I'm sorry, I didn't understand what you said." Alexa gave her standard response when hearing a non-programmed order.

Chuckling at "her" confusion, and remembering that for all her smarts, she was still only rudimentary AI, Daniel reverted to a standard command. "Alexa, play music."

"Here's a song I think you might like." 'She' paused before adding, "Babe."

This elicited a guffaw from Daniel, but then a plaintive child's voice started singing from the Echo. He quickly recognized the song "Calling Occupants of Interplanetary Craft." But instead of The Carpenters this cover was by The Langley School Music Project. As the chorus of grade school kids began Daniel, eyes watering, nibbled at his meal.

At first, he feared the brightness would blind him but then realized he could look at it quite easily without pain. Daniel was out of body again, only this time instead of the eerie astral twilight the room was flooded from overhead with an intense white light. Mesmerized, he floated into the shaft of light and was engulfed in an oceanic feeling. A white fog surrounded him as he lost all earthly bearings and felt the presence of other souls in the impenetrable atmosphere. But there was no real separation between them; each soul he knew was part of a whole like a ripple on water, or a wave on an ocean. And that ocean was Source.

Then miraculously the fog coalesced into matter, and he was immediately in another realm. He stood on the floor of an immense cathedral rotunda more than 1000 feet in diameter. The dome above was supported by a gold ring of Corinthian Greek columns, their bases the girth of giant sequoias in a first growth forest, their ornate voluted capitals under girded by richly veined acanthus leaves. As his eyes followed the tall columns up, he luxuriated in an intricately painted ceiling, perhaps 1000 feet or more, like nothing he could have imagined, a dome of heaven that seemed to disappear into infinity. But so intricate and complex was it that he wondered how any man or group of artists, even an army of Michelangelos, could have created such a masterpiece that put the Sistine Chapel to shame, could have achieved such a byzantine mosaic of intertwined figures, for it seemed the units composing the artwork were human figures spiraling upward in perfect perspective to a common point at the apex of the dome, an intense white point of light, radiating out and downward, similar to the light he had slipped into. When he looked at the point of light, he saw with more than his eyes, in many dimensions, in a sense became the point and understood that the beings were melding into each other from all directions, like a black hole's gravity pulls in everything around it. That was it! It was a black hole, but white, all colors joined together.

As he stared at the wondrous, awe-inspiring spectacle, he suddenly realized it was not a static work at all. It was moving! The individual beings were real, and alive...living art. Somehow, he was able to look closer just by thinking it, as if his eyes were binoculars or zoom lenses, and the mass of bodies resolved into individual entities...and they were not all human beings! In fact, there were very few humans in the mass of life all moving toward a common destination. Alien beings: Greys, Tall Whites, Mantis, Reptilian, Nordics, and many bizarre species he'd never seen before or could have imagined. And animals, large and small. All life was represented in this massive flux of living energy – wildebeest, elephants, bison, panthers, tigers, orangutans, meerkats, dogs and cats, robins and starlings, and insects, ants, bees, spiders, scorpions, cockroaches, beetles, and fish of the oceans, dolphins, whales, octopi, barracudas, tuna, trumpetfish, even tiny krill and reptiles of all kinds, snakes, poisonous and non, lizards, frogs, salamanders, all were represented and entwined, none in competition or fighting, even if it was their nature to do so, each in harmony with its neighbors, traveling to a common terminus, the white light of creation, the Source. Nature in full representation. There was no animosity or fear, only joy, peace, and tranquility, in the intricately entwined aggregation. And most important of all, everything radiated love. Unconditional love. Daniel felt it. Love, yes, love was the glue that held this mass of life together.

As he gazed in wonder, his body rose to the level of the column capitals, to where the lowest figures were just beginning their journey. New beings seemed to manifest from the curved stone architrave that connected the column tops, an endless source of souls migrating from physical life to the afterlife. As he stood on the outside observing, some of the mass reached out to him, hands, hooves, legs, tentacles, beckoning him in, to join the throng. They spoke in his mind, welcoming him in familiar terms as if they knew him.

"Is this Heaven?" he asked.

The beings answered. "We are a representation of your mind, what you have conceived of as Heaven."

"You are not real?"

"We are very real but appearing to you in a familiar form. To those of different belief and experience we might take another form."

"But you are so many."

"We are infinite. We are One. For this lesson we are as we were in our most recent incarnation."

As he gazed at the flow of beings a longing consumed him and he wanted to go with them, knew someday he would be in that mass naturally migrating back to Source…but his time was not now. He still had work to do in the material world, on Earth.

With that thought, Daniel was back in his own bed at the

cabin, fully awake and beside himself with joy at the marvel he'd just witnessed.

Jesse at his feet, Daniel now slept soundly, when the darkened room suddenly filled with bright light streaming in from outside and the atmosphere vibrated with a muffled "whump, whump" emanating from the sky over the cabin. Daniel was awake now, alarmed and confused. This light from outside was harsh and hurt his eyes. Daniel threw off the covers and was getting up when the door slammed open and 3 black-clad military troopers burst into the room. Jesse lunged to protect Daniel but there was a sharp electrical snap and he fell limp from a wand-like device wielded by one of the soldiers.

"Jesse!" screamed Daniel, but before he could get to his pet the intruders were on him, forcing him back down on the bed. As he fought their restraints, he too was zapped by a trooper with another device. He felt an electrical tingle before he lost all muscle control. Unable to move, his eyes revealed his terror as the team quickly lifted him out of bed and forced him into body bag attached to a stretcher. One of the troopers zipped it up, leaving just enough opening for his face so he could breathe. Then they carried him outside to the clearing next to the cabin where a Stealth Black Hawk helicopter hovered above the pines. A hoist line and harness awaited the stretcher and soon he found himself swaying in the cool night air as he was lifted into the craft.

The lone helicopter raced across the night desert landscape toward the Chocolate Mountains in the distance. It slowed for descent into a hidden valley where there was a secluded military base far from any city or town. The chopper set down on a camouflaged pad before an open hangar door. The hangar

CHAPTER 13

itself was built into the side of the mountain perfectly hidden from overhead reconnaissance satellites. Daniel, still on the stretcher, was carried inside.

The hangar, a vast space where numerous aircraft were housed, including saucer craft of different sizes and shapes, was like a UFO museum. The team's path took them past two of the craft. By design, i.e., following orders, they slowed down to make sure Daniel saw the contrasting craft. One rested heavily on a tripod of landing gear, a German Haunebu-type saucer with riveted panels and gun barrels protruding from the upper turret dome. But the other hovered off the floor and was breathtaking, a gleaming seamless metal saucer perhaps 50 feet in diameter that emitted a blue phosphorescent glow. The abduction team continued with Daniel to a large freight elevator and rode to the depths below.

Alone in a darkened room, Daniel was now strapped to an examination table. A door opened, silhouetting a single figure against the bright light from outside the room. As the figure moved in a thick reptilian tail dragged the floor behind. The dark figure loomed over a panicked Daniel, pulling frantically against his restraints, while menacing yellow eyes with black vertical slits set in a scaly forehead stared down at him mercilessly. Just then 3 uniformed men entered the room and the figure stepped back before the overhead light switched on. Air Force Colonel McDonald spoke to Sergeant Butterfield before directing his attentions to Daniel.

"Sergeant, let's free up the Professor here." The sergeant released the straps that bound Daniel, allowing him to sit up.

"Professor James, I'm Colonel McDonald. I see you've met Captain Rocco." Daniel followed the captain's bob of the head and did a double take upon seeing a conventional human Air

Force officer, Captain Rocco, standing where the Reptilian being had been just moments ago.

Noting Daniel's consternation, Captain Rocco smiled wryly. "Professor."

Daniel was confused and, yet there was something about Captain Rocco that was familiar, as if they'd met before - perhaps a science conference? But given the turmoil that was going on in his mind at this moment - forcibly extracted from his bedroom to an underground military base somewhere and for what purpose? - he had no time to reflect on what it could have been.

"I imagine you're wondering why you are here."

Daniel wanted to scream his outrage at the colonel's low key, inane comment, but he managed somehow to keep his outward composure and simply ask. "Where's here?"

"That, I'm not at liberty to divulge."

"Alright, then why?"

"It's come to our attention that you may have witnessed a top-secret event in the desert."

"How…?" Daniel paused to choose his next words carefully. Somehow this colonel knew what happened at Joshua Tree or was fishing for an admission and information. Either way all Daniel's inward danger detectors screamed "caution." He maintained his cool. And like any good Socratic debater he answered with a question of his own. "Top secret? So, you're saying what I may, or may not, have witnessed was one of yours?"

"That's classified. Would you tell us exactly what you saw?"

So, the colonel was being coy. Two could play that game. "It's classified."

Colonel McDonald was not amused. "We're not playing

games here, professor."

"I think maybe that's exactly what you are doing. A very calculated, intimidation game. I mean, kidnapping me from my own home?"

"Would you have come if we asked nicely?"

"Under what pretense?"

"Look, professor, we have the right under provisions of the Espionage Act and the Patriot Act to investigate subversive activity."

"Subversive? I took a hike in the desert!"

"You've also been fraternizing with a subversive group."

"Oh, what group do you mean?"

"ET. Maxine Braun's organization."

"It's a support group. There's no law against people meeting to discuss common experiences."

"Look, I don't want to threaten you or yours, but certain elements of that group could be considered a threat to American security. I just want you to be aware of that. And it would be a great help to your country if you would let us know what goes on in those meetings."

"You want me to be a spy?"

"Let's not be overly dramatic about this. Just do your patriotic duty and let us know of anything suspicious."

"Like what?"

"Like plans for an invasion."

"Invasion? Are you serious? Colonel, you've seen too much science fiction."

The colonel's patience ran out. He motioned to a noncom nurse who stood behind Daniel. "Just remember what I said. We'll be in touch." The nurse placed a handheld device at the base of Daniel's skull. Instantly, he lost consciousness, falling back on the table where he was immediately re-strapped in and carted away.

Daniel awoke back in his bed, feeling stiff and very groggy. What a night! A night of contrasts! He vaguely recalled a beautiful, ethereal dream but also a horrid nightmare. When he reached down to pet Jesse, he discovered the bed was empty. He jumped out of bed calling for his dog when he heard a whimper from the corner of the bedroom. Jesse was there, cowering in the shadows. Daniel crouched down to pet him. "Boy, what's the matter? You're trembling." He hugged him tightly. "It's okay, Jess. Let's get you breakfast."

He had to pull Jesse up. The dog walked unsteadily like he too had been on a drunken bender.

Daniel started for the kitchen when his eyes were drawn to the floor. There were multiple muddy tracks coming down the hallway. He tracked them to the front door now standing wide open with the cool morning air chilling the cabin. He closed the door. It was real; he'd been taken last night. Down on the floor with his arms around Jesse again, he comforted him with new vigor. "Did they hurt you, Jesse?"

Chapter 14

Parked in the driveway, Daniel was just coaxing a limping Jesse out of his car as Melanie came to the door. Alarmed at the condition of her pet, she rushed out. "What happened to him?"

"I don't know. He's been this way all morning," Daniel stammered.

"Put him in my car. I'm taking him to the vet now!"

As he explained Jesse's condition to the couple in the small office waiting room, the vet's tone was grave. "I've given him a sedative so he's sleeping. I think it's best I keep him overnight to make sure he doesn't manifest any more symptoms."

"Do you know what's wrong with him?" asked Melanie.

"He acts like he's been through some trauma. Do you know what?"

They both shook their heads. The vet went on, "I found two marks on his back. They look like electrical burn marks to me."

Melanie whipped around to glare at Daniel, who registered genuine shock.

"I don't know how that could have happened," he said. "He was inside all night. And he was fine when we went to bed."

As the two walked to their cars, Melanie was having none of

Daniel's equivocating. "Daniel, what aren't you telling me?"

Daniel regarded the pavement and fidgeted. "Melanie, we need to talk."

Sometime later, Melanie and Daniel sat in a quiet corner at a nearby diner. Melanie stared at her coffee mug in disbelief. "Jesus, Jesus, Jesus."

"It's a lot to take in," Daniel said, sympathetically.

Melanie's response was scathing. "Alien mother ships, black…something… military, secret underground bases… Are you out of your mind? Or do you think I am?"

"It's fantastic, I know. But there is a logic to my speculation."

Melanie shot him a withering look.

"Jesse would have tried to protect me last night from the soldiers. Who else would have used such a device on him?"

"I don't know what is going on with you, Daniel. I don't know what the truth is. But somehow you have put our baby at risk when you should have protected him!"

"Melanie, I had no idea this would happen…and I was paralyzed!"

She started to cry. "I can't lose him, too."

Daniel reached across the table to take her hand, but she pushed him away, got up and ran from the diner. Daniel started after her but halted on reaching the door to watch in futility as she climbed into her car and drove off. He returned to his seat and sat staring into space.

In a small examination room with Dr. Sylvia Cybele, a sixtyish reproductive endocrinologist, Daniel and Melanie waited nervously while Dr. Cybele scanned a report.

"Everything looks normal, except Daniel's sperm count is

somewhat low," she said. "This is not unusual. Remember, in 40 – 50 percent of couple's infertility, the male is responsible. This does not mean a pregnancy is impossible, but it will take diligence, a little luck and some techniques we can help you with."

She turned to the couple and spoke sternly. "Daniel, Melanie. I don't want either of you to get discouraged. Remember it only takes one successful 'swimmer' to complete the task. Be positive. Make it fun."

At first, they tried everything suggested by Dr. Cybele and then some.

- Daniel sweated profusely while running on a treadmill as Melanie walked through the room with a basket of laundry under one arm. "Just getting my swimmers in shape," he huffed. She gave him a thumbs up.

- Daniel worked with his notebook computer resting on his lap. A stern looking Melanie stood before him with a couch pillow. He sheepishly lifted the computer up, and she placed the pillow underneath as a buffer. "Keep those family jewels cool, honey bunch."

- Melanie sat on the toilet reading an ovulation strip as Daniel brushed his teeth at the sink beside her. Suddenly she exclaimed, jumped up and grabbed him by the arm, barely giving him time to spit, before dragging him out the door. In the bedroom they flopped on the bed, ripping their clothes off like two virgins in heat.

This, one could say, almost feverish activity of preparation went on for months to no avail. Finally, they decided a drastic change of scenery was needed for a while, if for nothing else than to relieve them of what they called "preparental pressure."

With Daniel's vacation coming up, they chose to vacation in Hawaii and made reservations on Maui, a cottage on the beach complete with single mast outrigger sailboat.

Daniel had loved sailing since his undergraduate days at Long Beach State, where he'd taken to it readily after only a few months of lessons, becoming proficient enough to sail a 32-foot Newport solo to Catalina off the California coast. Soon he was giving lessons himself to supplement his scholarship for spending money.

He enjoyed the history of sailing navigation and its connection to the stars, amazed at how early Polynesian and Micronesian sailors had used the heavens and knowledge of the sea to sail routes all over the Pacific, thousands of miles without charts or even minimal equipment like a sextant and compass. One story intrigued him. An illiterate Micronesian navigator had been put to the extreme test by a modern schooner captain when he covered his compass and let his primitive peer guide them to Saipan, an 1100-mile round trip, and a place the navigator had never been to, nor had any of his fellow sailors going back many generations. But the means to get there, navigating by the stars, was embedded in his craft's oral history and he was confident he could guide his friend there without fail. They showed up in Saipan a week later.

So, Daniel was pleased now to finally kill two birds with one stone and sail while on vacation with his beautiful Melanie.

The environment of Hawaii was especially sensual and erotic. The warm tropical breezes, the thin film of moisture that seemed to never leave your skin. The baring of one's body to the elements, night or day. The smells, tastes, sounds were all so exotic…and sexy. Surely these surroundings were the perfect setting for the most creative of human endeavors, the making of another human being, forged in love in the most caressing and erotic of environs.

The indigenous people of the Pacific had known it for millennia. Polynesian women were trained in the art of lovemaking as were Micronesian women. In fact, there was the legendary love school on Truk. Dubbed the University of the Arts of Love by the Americans when it was US Trust Territory, who were never certain of its existence, the Truk love school was a finishing school for sex training and had been driven underground by missionaries since the early contact period. Quite simply, older women taught young girls, average age fourteen, how to please a man. The training, however, did not include men and guards were posted to keep them out. Graduates were coveted all over the Pacific as wives and the phrase, "She's a Truk girl," carried a similar cultural status to "She's a Radcliffe girl" in America.

All day they had been preparing for a night at sea, the last night before they must depart their tropical paradise. Daniel's plan, conveyed to Melanie at dinner the night before, was to sail out in the early afternoon, far enough to elude even the minimal lights of civilization on Maui, lash the rudder, roll the sails, and set out the sea anchor, a device to produce maximal drag in the water, since they would be too far out into the deep sea for a bottom anchor, and thus keep a sailboat in relatively stable position. Without the need to tend the sailing of the craft they would be free to make love, and a baby, all night with only the sensations of the sea to tend them.

Once under sail, though, the warm western breeze was gentle and soon departed entirely, leaving the sails limp, so Daniel motored on until land was beyond the horizon. A spectacular sunset on a knife-edge horizon and the sky was quickly dark as only unpolluted air can deliver. They dined on simple fare by candlelight, sharing a drinking coconut. Immature coconuts not only contained liquid "water" that quenched thirst but also provided calories and nutrients. Oftentimes Daniel had drained a coconut in lieu of a meal and was able to function with the energy level of ingesting more substantial food. Tonight, they completed their meal by Daniel cracking the nut's shell with back edge of a machete, striking it midpoint alternately on opposite sides until it split open, after which they scooped out its gelatinous lining of immature coconut meat with spoons as an adjunct to their liquid meal.

Dousing the candle, they crawled out onto the webbing of the outrigger and waited as the stars emerged fully.

Sitting quietly in the starlight, they felt a swell roll the canoe, a rising undulation hidden beneath the surface of the flat sea that only revealed itself when under them. As he watched the craft move, Daniel felt it glide to the other side and saw a spot of light in it. A light in the sea? He looked closer and saw other small reflections in the oily smooth surface. He looked overhead and was awed by the night. The sky was alive with points of light, some large and bright, others, shadowy figures at the edges of his sight that disappeared with a direct look. Spatters of celestial paint on a black canvas, in places only a profusion of random dots, but in others a pattern was clear as if guided by the hand of an artist. No longer merely a black and white firmament, there were colors he had never seen, subtle hues of red, blue, and yellow in the suns and planets that hung there, and all seemed within reach. He experienced the night's splendor to its fullest extent upon the globe, uncut by land in the full circle of the horizon, no cloud or wisp of mist to obscure, no garish city tungsten glow in the distance, no second-hand sun, the vulgar moon, to overwhelm. Only stars, stars, stars. Stars that radiated a glow perceptible in their totality, a soft friendly glow, not cold and impersonal, the stuff of textbooks and star charts and maps of the heavens, but a living sky, a personal sky, his sky, their sky.

Daniel's hands beheld Melanie's gentle, open face in starlight and he kissed her tenderly on the lips. He unbuttoned her blouse and slipped it off, exposing her to the faint cool breeze. She yielded, even though a feeble reticent modesty still tugged at her conscience. He took the plug from a hollow coconut and poured the oil in his hands, and gently worked it into Melanie's neck and shoulders, a deep massage that soothed and tingled. The sweet aroma rose and caressed their nostrils, evoking an ethereal mood, a bliss that was erotic. The combination of odor and touch melted the last of her inhibitions and she slipped out of her salt-stiffened Bermuda shorts and panties. The breeze on her loins was simply the most natural of aphrodisiacs, the baring of one to the gentle elements, the tantalizing eroticism of freedom.

Daniel massaged the entire length of her. She cupped her hands and he understood and filled them with the elixir, and she began a sensual massage of his body. Soon they were enclosed in an aromatic cloud, like a fragrant, fragile coconut bubble that sealed their skin from the breeze.

They lay together on the outrigger of the canoe on the woven mats Daniel had brought for their comfort, and from a wadded towel he fashioned a pillow for her head. The fiber of the mat was coarse but stimulating against their skin. They felt each other, slick and moist and warm, through the coconut oil membrane that was like another skin. His hands now changed from the firm supple massage to the light touch of caressing velvet. Her nipples became hard and erect as his lips brushed over them and he felt himself grow.

Time became irrelevant. Their bodies alertly awaited a new beginning, came in touch with their own cosmic energy, an electric potential drawn from the stars, an awakening of power, of strength, that dislodged the many anchors that held them below the surface of the sea of life. Their souls, like buoys storm-driven into depths beyond the length of their moorings, strained against their shackles for the surface far above.

As she took him in, her muscles responded, and he felt a rolling grip from stem to tip, tip to stem. He wanted to crawl completely into her body, to become her and she to become him. The coconut bubble expanded, and the buoy rose steadily, stretching the anchor ropes.

Their movements met the sea's, and the swells quickened. There was a sense of a great building, an expectation of wonder just at hand, rising and falling to the rhythm of the sea, to the pulse of the universe…and the expectation of a great coming.

Electricity that filled Melanie's body became waves of pleasurable fire, radiating outward from the pelvic nerves, focusing all concentration there, and coursed to her head. Her heart became a hummingbird's, the pressure of blood in her pelvis doubled, tripled, went off the scale. Her brain became a globe of light, and the light seemed to pass between them, as if they shared the same source.

Joyful spasms rocked her body and she arched her back to meet his thrusts, exploding her consciousness, as a giant swell carried them to the heights of pleasure, a great continental swell that they saw in their mingled minds, saw its evolution, its birth upon the American continent, a reflection of the sea's energy, traced its journey to Hawaii, building strength and momentum to lift them at that moment, propelling them to ecstasy on its crest, an immense rolling wave that lofted them to the stars.

Daniel and Melanie felt a weight lift from their consciousnesses, the anchors that held their emotions were gone, dissolved by the electricity and light, the buoy of their beings bobbed free in the sea, free now to float with the currents, to explore the latitudes of serene doldrums or perhaps be dashed on a rocky coast, but free, finally, to choose, to experience, and to create, life.

Their bodies fused for a moment without defenses. The sheer ecstasy of sharing caused her to cry out for joy, to open her eyes to the splendor overhead, to Daniel's windswept profile outlined against a ceiling of stars, as the salt from her own sea oozed from her pores and mixed with his sea and the oils of the primal coconut, in the magical alchemy of love creating a singular elixir of them.

Then they were at peace, a tender loving state, when self is only part, and fulfillment can only be in giving to another. She shifted her body on the pliant webbing of the outrigger and he slid in beside her and smiling, kissed her gently on the lips, touching velvet again, and closed his eyes.

She watched him sleep far into the night, and watched the stars gently glide overhead as the dark pulsating ocean rolled and felt the new full power of being, till sleep overwhelmed her too. As the couple lay entwined in peaceful repose, the timeless heavens peering down on them, oblivious to all that encompassed their tiny craft, the ocean's immense breadth below mirroring the firmament above, one of the stars suddenly brightened…and moved.

Twilight awakened them. The stars, their guides, and compatriots in love, had vanished, leaving them alone in the vast sea, but Melanie was not frightened. She now trusted him completely.

They bathed in the sea, naked bodies exposed as never before, completely free of inhibition and they wanted to cast away clothing forever. The sea was warm and invigorating, and felt so natural, so familiar, so filled with amniotic memory of another womb, which too had once made them feel this new and fresh and alive.

He was aft, naked, yellow towel wrapped around his neck like an aviator's scarf trailing in the breeze. He grinned at her, lying in the pastel orange of the early sun and she was not ashamed by her own body. Sea birds, noddys and terns, squalled, winging their way to sea for the day after roosting last night on land. Their land. Daniel raised the sail, the wind had come up in the early morning, and steered a course in the direction from which the birds came. She didn't have to ask but understood his purpose. As they coursed through the rising seas, picked up by the wind with the ascending sun, their spirits soared like the sea birds. Over the horizon they knew was Maui.

They watched as a speck grew in the distance, coming toward them in the air. Giant wings unfurled, soaring ever closer. It made for them, their little floating island, and settled its broad expanse on the outrigger. An albatross, a good omen from the sea, the ancient bird had come to witness their union. They didn't speak, not a word since last night, but shared the experience in smiles and gestures until the old one lifted off again, his giant wings catching the wind to fly into the west.

CHAPTER 14

On the flight home, they both slept as people do when suddenly released from a long taxing physical ordeal, or at a long and arduous mental task's end, dropping into deep slumber as the wheels of the 747 left the Honolulu tarmac until they touched again with a thump and skid at LAX.

The return to their routines was seamless. But they both sensed that something was different now, a carefreeness had infected them both. Sidd noticed it immediately as their playful banter of bachelorhood seemed to have returned.

"I believe the worm has turned for you, my friend," he told Daniel and poured another shot of mescal, then observed the agave worm settling again in the bottom of the bottle. Daniel acknowledged the benediction with a nod before a quick downing of his own shot and the lime wedge chaser.

"It was magical, Sidd, even spiritual. Whatever happens, I think we both can accept the outcome knowing we gave it our all."

"Amen, bro."

A few weeks later as Daniel walked down the path toward the Palomar office building, his phone pinged. He paused to look at the text. On screen was a selfie of a screaming Melanie, with the words, "We're having a baby!" Daniel screamed himself and danced an impromptu jig while pumping his fist in the air. "YES! YES! Super swimmer!" An Asian tour group noticed his "crazy American" antics and soon cameras and smart phones were raised in his direction, recording and sharing as TikTok and Facebook videos.

Three months later, Melanie and Daniel lounged in bed with

Daniel feeling playful, "Hey, momma-to-be, has our little Ziggy moved yet?"

"Stop calling him Ziggy. SHE's our little embryo now. And I told you, it's too early for movement."

"Sez you, first timer. I happen to know from high authority that our kid is an embryonic prodigy."

"Higher authority than me?"

"Oh, yes. From the little pony's mouth HERself. And it's time for an update." Melanie laughed as Daniel lay his ear over her baby bump to listen. She lovingly stroked his head. "Well?"

"Oh, my. She's venting. Something about…'Damnit…' Actually, she said, 'Darn it,' but I embellish. 'Damnit, lay off the rum raisin ice cream and pickled garlic.' It makes her retch."

"Makes YOU retch!"

"No. No. This is not about me. And, SHE says, 'What's all the bouncing around in the morning. How's a kid to get any rest?'"

"Yeah, you want to explain about your morning 'needs'?"

"I think she might be too young for that, don't you?" Daniel raised up to gaze expectantly at his wife. She smiled back, invitingly. He glanced at the digital bedside clock. "Past midnight. It's morning!" He reached over and switched off the light as they fell together passionately.

Piercing the darkened bedroom, a light switched on in the bathroom. Suddenly, Melanie screamed. Daniel leaped out of bed and rushed into the bathroom where he found Melanie standing in a blood-stained nightgown.

Daniel shuddered at the remembrance of that night, the rush to the ER and then the long wait until the doctor confirmed that

CHAPTER 14

the baby was lost. All the promise that had awaited them and their lives in the impending birth of their child, dashed in one fell swoop. Would their union, imperfect though it was, ever recover? Not likely, he knew, unless he could find some proof, physical proof to convince Melanie. After today it would have to be beyond reproach; the odds were against that. He slowly rose and left the diner.

Chapter 15

As Daniel walked across the parking lot, he noticed two men hovering around his Polestar. Both were young toughs, hard types with military buzz cuts in civilian dress. Since he owned an unfamiliar and exotic sports car, he was used to passers-by checking it out, so assumed they were curious about his electric vehicle. But on seeing him approach, they quickly backed away to their own vehicle double parked across from his, a black SUV, like the one Daniel had seen at the cabin. Odd behavior, thought Daniel, suspicions aroused, as he climbed into the driver's seat; they continued to watch him intently. He switched the EV on, but the familiar hum of the engine starting did not follow, instead the screen flashed a warning "Batteries: No charge." In astonishment he looked at the young toughs, both smirking back at him.

Infuriated, Daniel jumped out and started toward them. "Hey! What'd you do to my vehicle?"

Immediately, the SUV pulled away with a squeal of rubber. Daniel ran in pursuit until they cleared the lot and turned onto the main road. He watched helplessly as they disappeared into traffic.

Luckily, an auto club tow truck had been available and dispatched promptly; within the hour he was at an EVcharging station. A 20-minute rapid charge on the dead system would be enough, he reasoned, to get him to the cabin where overnight he could get his batteries properly replenished on his own system.

As he waited for the truck, he had plenty of time to assess what had happened. Did the two men really drain his batteries remotely? Was that even possible? He knew there were devices that could be charged wirelessly, so it was reasonable to assume they could be discharged in the same manner. And who were they? Black ops agents or perhaps operatives from Dr. Bains's Astralis organization? He'd have to be more careful and watchful in the future.

But his more immediate concern was Melanie. Clearly, she doubted his explanation for Jesse's condition. And could he blame her? Just a few short months ago such talk of aliens and secret military abductions would have sent him fleeing the source of such nonsense. And Mel had always been more open to the bizarre, spiritual, and psychic phenomena, than he. As a trained Reiki practitioner, she dealt in subtle energy as a way of life. He had always had doubts about her craft on the intellectual level of a scientist, but on a heart level he'd always believed his wife understood much of reality far better than he. As his love for her clouded his rational judgment at times, in irrational matters involving her he learned to simply suspend judgment. It was part of the duality of male/female relationships, indeed, like the one half of life, and human beings, that Western science chose to ignore but that the East had always embraced, yin/yang, opposites coexisting side by side, each containing the seed of the other.

In the Hale Observatory data room, Daniel sat at a computer

console programming a future operation of the 200-inch telescope. Sidd entered from the dome room. "You about finished?"

"Just putting the final touches on the run. Then it's all yours."

Daniel made a few on screen adjustments, then hit enter. As he rose to let Sidd take his seat, his cell phone rang. He picked up to hear a frantic Melanie on the other end. "He's gone! Daniel, I can't find him anywhere."

"Who's gone, Melanie?"

"Jesse! He ran off as I was getting ready to give him a bath."

"Okay, I'm leaving now!"

"What's wrong, buddy?" Sidd inquired.

Daniel ran for the door. "Melanie is frantic. Jesse ran off." And he was gone.

"He'll come back when he gets hungry enough." Sidd shouted to the empty room, then added softly to himself. "You'd think he was their kid."

When Daniel arrived and been apprised of the situation - Jesse had run into the adjacent woods while Melanie was filling the plastic kiddie pool they sometimes used to bath him in warm weather - they agreed to split up to better cover the large area that their dog had fled to and where he was now likely hiding in fear. They separately walked through woods and field calling for Jesse. By dusk their efforts had proved fruitless, and they retired to the house - Melanie readily agreed to let Daniel stay the night in the guest bedroom but not before he felt compelled to ask. The next morning Daniel stapled a reward poster with Jesse's picture to several telephone poles in their Escondido neighborhood, having designed them with a picture, description, and $100 reward the night before. The reward

CHAPTER 15

was probably not necessary in the affluent neighborhood but might be enough to incentivize the local kids in the search.

The next afternoon, the couple sat in dejection around the kitchen table. Melanie was particularly distraught. "It's been two days. I think he's…I think…" She couldn't bring herself to say what was becoming more and more evident with each passing day: that their pet had met with a fate they did not want to contemplate.

"Don't, Melanie. We'll find him." Daniel gamely tried to remain upbeat. He grabbed the phone book from off a shelf under the landline phone. "I'm calling the county animal shelters. Maybe they picked him up because of he didn't have a collar." He was staring at Jesse's collar on the kitchen counter which Melanie had removed in preparation for his bath.

Later Daniel was just hanging up the phone as Melanie walked in. From his look she became immediately alarmed. "What's wrong, Daniel? Did you find him?"

"A golden lab was brought in two days ago."

"Could it be him? Let's go right now."

"No. Melanie, he was hit by a car and injured."

"Well, let's go. He needs us. We've got to get him the proper treatment."

"They…they put him down. It's their policy. If the animal is suffering and can't be IDed, they're euthanized. They thought he was a stray."

"No, no, no." She began to cry. "Maybe it wasn't him. You go, Daniel, go and see if it was our baby. Go!"

"I can't."

"I've got to know. Maybe it wasn't him. Why are you resisting? Go! Go now!"

Daniel spoke sharply, "Melanie!" Then softly, "They…

cremated him."

This hit Melanie like a brick to the head. She slumped in her chair and just stared at the space in front of her. Daniel came round to softly stroke her neck and shoulders. For the first time in months, she didn't refuse his touch.

In a darkening room lit only by the fading light from outside, Melanie and Daniel silently sat with their thoughts. Suddenly Melanie shouted, "I hate helicopters!"

Daniel looked up, perplexed by the outburst.

"I know it was that fucking helicopter." Melanie continued.

"What are you talking about, Mel?"

"One of those damned Marine helicopters flew low over the house just before he bolted. I think it scared him."

Daniel's face reflected his realization. "You're right, Mel. Jesse was traumatized by those men and their helicopter that night at the cabin. Of course, he would have been frightened to think it was happening again."

For Melanie too a realization dawned, that what Daniel had said was responsible for Jesse's injury, might be true, fantastic as it was to believe.

Meanwhile rage was building in her husband the likes of which she'd never seen. Daniel pounded his fist on the table. "They're responsible for this, the colonel and his black ops troops! And now it's cost us Jess." The words choked in his throat. He paced the floor, wanting to do something, frustration building. He beat his fists on the table repeatedly until Melanie came over to wrap her arms around him. He calmed then and turned to the refuge of her arms.

"I believe you," she whispered.

III

Part Three

Perhaps everything that frightens us is in its deepest
being something helpless
that wants our love.
Fear of the Inexplicable, Rainer Maria Rilke

Chapter 16

Daniel reclined in a chair next to Maxine as she prepared him for hypnosis. "Now you are completely relaxed, Daniel. I want you to go back to that place and time, that night in the desert…"

Daniel, Byron, and Hoshi stood under the mother ship, gazing up at the radiant underbelly like deer in a headlight. Around each of them were two Grey aliens – short, bald humanoids with huge black teardrop eyes - who guided them in their trance state.

A flash of intense white light projected a wide beam onto each one of them in turn until it got to Daniel. As the beam engulfed him, Daniel, in a paralyzed state, rose weightless into the ship.

Daniel was now in a full hypnotic state, reliving the events of that night. As he spoke his agitation increased. "I'm enclosed in light. I can't see anything but white, white light. It's so bright it hurts my eyes. I'll go blind!"

The light beam turned off and Daniel, still levitated, now moved into a horizontal position as he floated over to a flat examination table. His body was still paralyzed but his eyes were not, and they quickly darted around the room, frantically trying to gain bearing.

"I can't move. The room is white and the walls are curved. I can't see any straight lines or flat spaces. I can't get my bearings."

The ceiling and walls faded away and he was in deep space with brilliant stars shining all around.

"It's like I'm floating at the center of the universe with stars everywhere. They're beautiful! But I don't recognize anything, no constellations, none of the familiar asterisms. Where am I?"

One of the golden stars began to grow in size and intensity and moved over Daniel.

"I feel…love, such pure intense love. There's a voice in my head. It's the orb."

"Daniel, I'm your spirit guide for this lifetime." Before Daniel, the orb took human shape, a beautiful angelic being hovering over him.

"Souls have no names," she continued, "for it's not necessary in spirit; we know each by our energy signature. Only your present ego requires a name. We've known each other for many incarnations. But each time to complete your Higher Self's purpose we switch on abilities according to the physical entity's needs. Your ability to travel out of body in the astral plane will be enabled. Psychic abilities will also be activated. Your soul agreed to this before incarnating. And now it's time to play out your part, as father to your child."

The golden angel placed one hand on Daniel's head and one over his heart. Presently, his astral body emerged to float above his matter form that now appeared to sleep.

CHAPTER 16

"I'm free, all bodily pain is gone. This must be what death is like, a freeing of the flesh to carry on in spirit. I could stay this way forever. But she told me I couldn't."

"It is not time for you to transition, Daniel. You still have work to do on Earth. But remember this moment whenever you feel fear. All fear is but fear of death. And death is not to be feared. For the soul never dies."

"I know she's right. And I love her, love all of them. My star family. It's time for me to go back to play out my role."

Daniel was back on the ship's examination table; the stars and Spirit Guide had disappeared. There were small humanoid beings around him; they had large hairless heads with bulging black eyes and 3-fingered hands. From behind the small beings, a tall slender humanoid with insect features, a Mantis alien, stepped forward. He seemed to be in charge.

"I'm back in my body. This large insect is inside my head now. He tells me that I should listen to my friend. I don't know what he means. What friend?"

Another being now stepped into Daniel's line of sight. He was clad in a raiment of radiant white. Daniel recognized him.

"It's Hoshi. He means Hoshi. He's inside my head now. But I don't hear him. I just feel this wave of serenity come over me. I know I can trust Hoshi."

Maxine had been watching this with professional detached reserve, and now brought Daniel out of his trance. "Daniel,

I'm counting back from ten and when I reach one, you will be fully awake. Ten…" When Daniel was fully awake, she queried him, "How do you feel, Daniel?"

"Relieved. Like a huge weight is off my chest."

"Do you understand now what the encounter meant?"

"It explains some things, like my weird psychic episodes. And the astral dreaming…Now I know they must be real, the astral traveling my Spirit Guide spoke of. But she said, 'Be a father to your child.' We don't have any children and when the divorce is finalized…"

"Remember in other dimensions there is no time and space as we know it."

"So, she was speaking of the future?"

Maxine shrugged.

Chapter 17

In his Polestar, Daniel wound up the mountain highway to his cabin. The effortless acceleration, the tight handling in sharp turns and switchbacks, made the EV a driving pleasure. On a straight stretch a descending vehicle approached at a high rate of speed, putting Daniel on alert. As he watched closely, it suddenly cut over into his lane, challenging him to an impromptu game of "chicken." Just before their sure collision Daniel swerved onto the shoulder and braked hard, spinning out to a stop on a scenic turnout. He watched, shaken, as the vehicle, another blackout SUV, powered away.

The next day at Harbor House Restaurant, Daniel waited at the same table for Dr. Bains to arrive. He had done his research on Benjamin Bains and had learned some interesting facts about the man, especially when he was a promising young research physicist. Bains's name had popped up along with a research partner in a popular science magazine and a series of articles in the *New York Herald Tribune* from the 1950s. There was nothing unusual about that, all young science researchers were eager to publish or have their work written up by others in credible publications. What made this article interesting was the subject matter, gravity and antigravity technology. Bains and his partner were credited with discovering G-(gravity) particles! Yes, the article claimed they had discovered the actual source of gravity, the subatomic culprit responsible for the force that has coalesced matter into, well, the Universe. The article predicted that G-engines, as they developed, would literally change the world, making all internal combustion engines obsolete. Automobiles, airplanes, ships, power plants would operate cleanly with little or no fossil fuel consumption whatsoever. Quoting top names in Fifties aviation technology and manufacturing, the articles put a time frame of but a few years to have workable engines. But the G-engines never appeared, and by 1960 it was as if the discovery of antigravity itself had never happened.

Daniel's curiosity led to a book, *The Hunt for Zero Point*, by Nick Cook, who happened to be at the time of its writing the aviation editor of *Jane's Defense Weekly*, the premiere defense publication in the world. Cook had tracked down one of the principal players in the affair from Martin Aircraft Corp, George S. Trimble, but when Trimble found out what Cook was researching, he refused to talk with him and warned Cook to leave the subject alone for his own safety. This led to Cook going down the rabbit hole of black ops projects within the government, where he discovered an elaborate system of technology cover-up. The pattern went like this, a certain subject was researched with public financing until it was resolved one way or another, where it either became an historical failure, discarded to the trash bin of history, or it was successful, and another scenario completely unfolded. It went dark, to be further developed, and perhaps implemented, in secret with black budget money so that the public only learned about it when convenient for this shadow government…

or perhaps never at all. With a revolutionary technology like antigravity, which would render obsolete every internal combustion engine in the world, and overnight unbalance the fossil fuel-based economies of the world, it most assuredly went dark.

Daniel was certain Dr. Bains knew a lot more than Nick Cook about the subject and was determined to query him today.

Dr. Bains arrived and took a seat opposite. "I'm happy to see you, Daniel. You made the right decision."

"Right now, my career is everything to me."

"Wise choice."

"Tell me about Astralis Academy."

"We're a for-profit science organization dedicated to disclosure on terms that fit the agenda of our clients."

"What clients?"

"That's not for public dissemination. Strictly on a need-to-know basis."

"And I don't…"

Bains shook his head. "All in good time, Daniel."

"What will my job be?"

"You'll be an authoritative spokesperson from the scientific community. An on-call expert when we need someone to put out a fire of public fervor over a sighting or to verify a sanctioned story. In short, you'll downplay what doesn't serve our agenda and play up what does."

"And I'll be paid for this?"

"Rather generously. In fact, you'll receive a regular cash stipend, always with the verbal proviso that you report this income to the IRS." He winked. "However, we never submit and there is no paper trail. This is black budget money, Daniel, so you needn't worry about any blow back."

"Sounds like you've done this before."

"We have most of the top media players on board, plus a large bank of material experts from academia like yourself."

"So, I'll keep my present job?"

"Absolutely! Your position is important to your credentials. Dr. Sauer will retire one day and…let's just say, you'll be in a good position to succeed him…with our help."

"He's part of this also?"

Bains nodded. "In fact, in time you'll be encouraged to write a book on a particular subject of interest to us and go on the ufology lecture circuit. To be a featured speaker at this new Contact in the Desert event would greatly please our benefactors."

"Ben, I was hoping you could enlighten me on the subject of gravity, your expertise. Frankly, I saw your name referenced in a few articles on the discovery of G-particles back in the Fifties. The articles were definitive that you had solved the mystery of gravity. But then nothing came of it. What happened?"

"So, you've been doing your homework. That's good. I'd expect nothing less from a man of science. I'd be happy to tell you all about my early work in gravity, but not here. That's a conversation for another time, another place. The topic is highly classified."

"So, the article was true?"

"Again, all in good time."

"Then, perhaps you can help me with another question I've been trying to answer. The people I met in the desert by chance that day were only there because of the area's UFO history. It was the site of the George Adamski contact in 1952. I've researched Adamski and it seems he might have been a con man. His tales of Venusians and Martians are easily disproved with today's astronomical knowledge of our solar system. With all your expertise on the subject, what was he? A real charlatan or an elaborate hoax victim?"

Bains looked at him sympathetically, then chuckled. "Adamski was one of our early projects."

"One of your operatives?"

"In a way, yes. He wasn't on the payroll and I don't want to call him a 'useful idiot,' to use the spy jargon of the Cold War era, but he was complicit with us in our disinformation program. He had some 'contact,' but with Germans posing as alien beings, the Nordics, and a captured saucer craft from WWII. He even rode in one of those ships. I believe he actually boarded a mother ship, one of the cigar-shaped variety you've no doubt read about. He had seen and experienced much of what he told about so that he was extremely believable and made a successful spokesman for our brand of the truth."

"But why would you encourage him to tell a story you were trying to hide?"

"A good way to hide the full truth is through a well-portrayed half-truth, or the believable lie. In 1947, we knew, after the commander of the Roswell base had let the cat out of the bag by his accurate press release, that enough people would start looking for an alien presence on Earth to make full containment impossible. We decided to encourage the contactees' wild tales and even planted our own narrative through contactees like Adamski, counter stories that would feed the need to believe in the gullible but would be easily debunked by the more discriminating. My favorite was always the Ozark farmer Buck Nelson and his Space dog Bo," he laughed mischievously, "who claimed to have traveled to the

Moon, Mars, and Venus to bring back 'God's Twelve Laws,' a modern equivalent of the Ten Commandments. His 'Moses' act brought a yokel quality to the genre that appealed to the Southern evangelical believers but had everybody else in stitches at his absurdities.

"As the contactees stories developed and became more outlandish, as the players competed for press, we hoped such 'incredible' stories and people would overshadow and discredit anyone trying to get the real story out. We polluted the jury pool of the court of public opinion, so to speak, for a generation or more. And it's worked perfectly."

"What about today? The contactees are almost entirely forgotten. I'd never heard of Adamski until I met those fellows in the desert."

"We continue our methods of psy-ops with operatives planted in the print media and elsewhere, Fox News, for example. The supermarket tabloids are especially effective for ridiculing any discovery or serious whistle-blower. Usually just the threat of having their story on a rag cover with say Hillary Clinton's alien baby is enough to give pause."

With that Dr. Bains rose, effectively terminating the meeting. Daniel walked with him out the restaurant door before they parted ways on the Embarcadero.

In San Diego's Tuna Wharf Park, Daniel strolled down the promenade near the famous "Unconditional Surrender Statue" a 3D rendering of an iconic 1945 photo by Alfred Eisenstaedt of a sailor dramatically kissing a nurse on V-J Day. In their courting days, Daniel remembered him and Melanie mimicking the famous couple in a friendly competition as Sidd and Deepa egged them on. Then it was Sidd and Deepa's turn and so on, back and forth, as each couple tried to out kiss the other. It was fun and they had even turned the tables on the action when Daniel playfully submitted to Melanie's passionate kiss, bending over backward like the nurse in the sculpture. The small crowd that had gathered to watch rewarded them with cheers, whistles and a few good-natured boos and catcalls.

On one of the benches ringing the plaza, Daniel spotted Peter, who waved him over. They sat with the USS Midway aircraft carrier, now a floating museum, behind them.

"Thanks for meeting me, Peter."

"What can I do ya for, my friend?"

"I'd like to pick your brain."

"Might be slim pickin's. But sure, go ahead."

"Do you know about any secret military operations, say staged abductions?"

"Wow, you plunge right in, don't you?" Suddenly cautious, Peter lowered his voice. "Let me put it this way: The military is very compartmentalized. Usually, you have your own area of involvement and are exposed minimally to anything outside that area. That said, people do talk - at lunch, you know - and they hint at things while not talking specifics. There was scuttlebutt about a unit that did carry out… 'unusual' missions like that."

"What's the purpose of faking alien abduction? I'd think the real thing would be scary enough."

"Most likely a false flag operation."

A man with a cap pulled low and dark sunglasses edged toward them with a camera to take a photo of the Midway. Daniel became nervous and stood, indicating with a bob of his head the intruder. "Let's take a walk." They moved out to the water's edge where there was less chance of their being overheard.

"So, what's a false flag operation?"

"Military history is full of incidents that were blamed on the enemy but, in fact, were orchestrated by friendly forces to force some action by armies or governments. The Gulf of Tonkin 'attack' during the Vietnam conflict was one. It got LBJ his war powers without going through Congress."

"Given that scenario, how do fake alien abductions make sense?"

"NASA is a civilian space agency, right? But, let's face it, the military calls the shots. And the military has long wanted to weaponize the space program, to protect Earth from attack from alien civilizations. Remember how Reagan famously said, the one thing that could unite the world would be an attack from outer space?"

"Oh, yeah."

"Well, presidents since then have echoed the same sentiment: Bush, Clinton, Obama. Then you had Trump signing a largely unnecessary United States Space Force Act into law. Something is afoot."

"How is that a bad thing?"

"The problem is it's a solution without a problem."

"How so?"

"We've been in contact with six alien civilizations and all of them are peaceful."

"Six civilizations! How would you know that?"

"Oh, don't take my word on it. That figure comes from Werner Von Braun, the head of our space program during the Apollo moon missions. He laid out a 4-point program that was being carried out to systematically instill fear in the American populace. We've been through three of them now, the last being an asteroid hitting Earth. Before that it was Russians, then international terrorism. Same old, same old. But the final fear factor will be…an invasion from outer space. That's how fake alien abductions make sense."

"But could it be justifiable? I mean if the goal is to protect us from a potential threat from space, couldn't a greater good come from this deception?"

"There just is no basis for fearing the alien races that have visited us. With the technology they have demonstrated, if conquest of Earth had been their goal, they could have accomplished that long ago. Rather, it seems, they want to help us evolve past the territorial, conqueror mentality that has dominated our history for thousands of years before we venture too far into space. Why do you think we stopped the space program after the Apollo moon landings?"

"As I recall we were told we just didn't have the money or the will of the people backing it with so many domestic problems at hand."

"Our government has proved over and over that money has never been a problem for a project they really wanted to do, especially if it involved defense. Rather, consider we were warned off the moon by alien civilizations that had been there for hundreds if not thousands of years."

"Are you saying there are alien bases on the moon?"

"Absolutely!"

"How could we not have seen them? We've had orbiters map every square foot of the moon, even the far side we never see from Earth."

"But we have seen them. And photographed them. During the National Press Club Disclosure conference in 2001 one of Steven Greer's experts testified he was shown undoctored high-res photos of the moon's surface while servicing equipment at NASA. He was secretly shown the original pictures of bases before they were air brushed out to hide them from the public…by the guy who was doing the doctoring. And consider this. Neil Armstrong revealed privately that during Apollo 11's famous moon walk they were watched by immense alien craft rimming the crater surrounding the Eagle LEM."

"I always thought that was just conspiracy theory."

"What about the ill-fated Apollo 13? It was carrying a small nuclear reactor to leave on the lunar surface. The mishap has never been satisfactorily explained, and all emphasis has been on the heroic efforts of the crew and support folks at NASA who saved them. The examples go on and on. We could even talk about all the mysteriously failed Mars expeditions."

"So, all this was calculated to keep us out of space beyond Earth's orbit until we proved what? That we are no longer an aggressive, warring species?"

"That's it in a nutshell."

"I wish I could be as sure of all this as you are, Peter."

"I have an idea that may help you. Why don't you come to a contact field trip with me next weekend? You'll meet people more knowledgeable about these things than me."

"I don't know, Peter. I'm trying to keep a low profile on this for now."

With that, Daniel bid goodbye to Peter. He had a lot to mull over. He'd often wondered himself why America's resolve to explore space, at least with manned missions, had evaporated with the end of the Apollo lunar program. But some of what Peter had claimed - Neil Armstrong an alien witness/advocate? - would have seemed preposterous, fodder for conspiracy lunatics, until a few weeks ago. Now he was a UFO witness himself. That bit of experience, like it or not, had changed his

CHAPTER 17

perception of reality…and the universe as he knew it, forever. Never again could he look up to the starry heavens with the cold detachment of an observer, a science version of a "just the facts, ma'am" Joe Friday. The night sky was no longer composed of raging hydrogen furnaces, gaseous giant planets, and barren rocky worlds. There was life out there. We were not alone. Not unique and not superior to all we observed. Man's dominion was confined to one tiny planet around one very average sun. Daniel James, PhD, was now a part of the opposition he'd fought against all his life.

Chapter 18

Like most people, Daniel hated spiders. His dislike was not an irrational fear; he did not suffer, as did 30 percent of his fellow Americans, from arachnophobia. It was just a general dis-ease, an unclean feeling at the thought of sharing his space with an 8-legged critter. When he saw a spider in his home, his first reaction had always been destruction, smash it flat, kill it quickly without another thought. That was then, now was different. Since Hoshi's cockroach intervention in the desert, he'd changed. How a simple command of "stop" in Japanese could have had such a profound impact on him was astonishing in retrospect. But now he simply did not think the same way about killing bugs, or killing anything, for that matter.

And it wasn't simply from Hoshi's emphatic directive. No, after ruminating on the desert incident and many odd occurrences since, he'd concluded that he was being retrained.

It began strangely. At first there were the spiders dropping into his face as he walked through the house. Suddenly, dangling on a silken string before his eyes was a spider. His instinctive response was to brush it away with his hand, then locate it on the floor so he could stomp on it. But there was never anything on the floor and he was left thinking perhaps he'd just imagined it. But if imaginary, the insect was real

CHAPTER 18

enough in the moment to make him physically react.

Then there were the long-legged spiders in the kitchen sink when he got up in the morning, frantically flailing for traction on the slippery porcelain side walls. The old Daniel would have washed them down the drain, but the post-desert Daniel carefully gathered each one in a plastic cup and released it outside in the woodpile. It was odd though. They would also appear in a stainless-steel mixing pan in the cupboard likewise unable to get traction to crawl out.Which posed the question: How did they crawl up the same smooth surface on the outside but now could not negotiate on the inside? And furthermore, upon release he would see them scamper out of sight behind a log. But when he looked to where they went, they were nowhere to be found. It was like they just disappeared.

Then they started showing up in the bathtub. He'd leave them alone for days, a week, as they spun webs, caught the little gnat-like bugs that seemed to be born out of the soil of the Ficus tree in the living room, the prey that sustained them. When a bath beckoned and he wanted to soak in Epsom salts, say after a long arduous workout at the gym, he would scoop them up and deposit them outside. Sometimes he would urge them onto a broom and walk them out only to have them scurry to the bottom side of the broom. But when he'd turn the broom over so that they didn't jump off onto the floor, they were gone. Just as he wondered out loud where they had gone, they would reappear, crawling back from the other side of the broom. Clearly something fishy was going on, yet he couldn't figure out what or why.

Then there was the final mystery spider that he believed had proven an otherworldly connection. At 2 AM one morning, he rose to use the toilet. A large spider raced down the wall behind him as he got up from the stool but, still in a sleep fog, he shrugged it off, and returned to bed. When he got up again at 4 AM, he heard a scratching sound from the high window curtains as the spider again came hurrying down the wall toward him. More alert now, he could see it was large, 2-3 inches long, and made an audible "shuffling sound" as it moved. Standing barefoot, clad in only boxer shorts, he, curiously, was not afraid of being bitten, but merely cautious as he intently watched the spider and sensed that the spider was watching him with equal interest and…intelligence.

After a long moment's scrutiny of Daniel, the creature crawled to the tile floor and went out under the door into the bedroom. This will not do, thought Daniel. I won't have him crawling around where I sleep. But when he looked for him in the bedroom, the spider was nowhere in sight. He kept a small LED flashlight next to his bed and used it to peruse his dumbbell rack loaded with the free weights he used for home exercises. And the spider was there, on the floor behind the legs of the workout bench. The bright light drove him up the wall to just under the ceiling where, as the glaring spot of light tracked him, he worked his way around the wall opposite Daniel's bed and turned the corner at the east wall's mirror closet doors. He's making for my bed, reasoned Daniel. This certainly will not do. As a deterrent, he turned on a torchiere floor lamp in the next corner ahead of the spider. When the area flooded with bright halogen light, the spider hesitated, seemed to reconsider, then turned and retraced his path down the wall to disappear under the door back into the bathroom. Determined to keep track of the critter, Daniel returned to the bathroom. Once again, he was nowhere to be found. I won't rest until I know where he's at, he grumbled silently, scanning the corners and shadows. Nothing. It was if yet another spider had disappeared into thin air. On a hunch he flipped over the white toilet rug that wrapped around the front of the stool to see if he was hiding underneath. Daniel was not prepared for what he found.

There on the white tile was a flattened gray "shadow" of the spider. It was clearly not a three-dimensional object, more like a silhouette without detail, as if someone had laid down a paper cutout of the insect to hold a place for the spider like a golfer places a dime on the green before lifting his ball off the grass. How strange, thought Daniel. I wonder if it phased out of this dimension for the time being. Before Joshua Tree he would not even have considered such a thing. But nothing was happening and clearly the shadow was a representation of the spider. His first thought was he could trap this two-dimensional thing for when it "came back" from wherever it now was. To this end, Daniel took a clear plastic cup from under the basin cabinet he often used to trap insects for removal from the house. Best be quick, he reasoned. In one swift movement Daniel engulfed the silhouette under the cup. Instantly, the shadow reconstituted into a real live spider that raced around the walls of the cup seeking escape. When it realized there was no escape, it stopped to peer up at Daniel.

"I don't really know what you are, my friend," he said out loud, "but I'm not going to hurt you. I'll take you outside later. But first I need proof that you are real." He transferred the critter to the dining room table by sliding a stiff piece of white paper underneath so he could lift the cup without providing a gap between cup and paper that its very alive and active contents could slip through. Then he took several photos from different angles with his digital SLR. When satisfied he had enough to identify the species, he decided to release his captive.

It was now daylight, past 5 AM, so he carefully carried the cup and paper outside and released the spider at the woodpile. Once free it scampered over the log and disappeared as Daniel knew it would. This time he didn't bother to look for it.

Now it fell on him to figure out what had just happened. What had that thing been? He never thought of keeping it captive while experimenting on it to perhaps force it to transform again. To the new Daniel, that would have been cruel, and he didn't consider it as the old scientist Daniel might have. What had the beings, that included insects, in his ethereal dream said? "We are infinite. We are One." It was enough to have seen the spider in a trans-dimensional state to convince him it was not a normal arachnid. It was controlled by an intelligent being, of that he was sure. And a being or beings that watched him and evaluated his actions. To what end? He had a guess. It was a test, he reasoned, a test of his value of life, all life, not just the higher forms like man. He was determined to pass this test.

Daniel was considering a theory; Other dimensions existed beyond our normal 3D (height, width, length) physical universe. How many? String theory, one of physics' most popular TOEs (theory of everything), posited 10-26 dimensions, depending on which variation, to make the complex mathematics work, the majority compactified out of this matter world so we didn't observe them. But what if at least one other dimension did exist alongside our normal 4D (since Einstein we've included space/time), and beings lived there and were capable

CHAPTER 18

of crossing over? Of course, much was still unexplained about the Universe. For instance, theoretically dark matter and dark energy, neither of which had been discovered experimentally, constituted 95% of the substance of the universe. He knew one model of string theory, Large extra dimensions (LED) theorized that our 4D universe floated on a membrane of 11D space. The forces of nature, electro-magnetism and the strong and weak nuclear forces, operated across the physical universe only but gravity operated over all 11 dimensions, thus accounting for its weakness *vis a vis* the other forces. Experiments at CERN and the Large Hadron Collider (LHC) had yet to reveal the postulated graviton's emergence…and disappearance, which would imply it had gone into one of the other dimensions. But the operational range of the LHC was too limited to cover the predicted range of the LED experiment.

Then there was the MIW, the Many Interacting Worlds theory, that came out of the opposition to the Copenhagen interpretation of quantum mechanics. The Copenhagen interpretation claimed the observer's consciousness created the collapse of the wave function enabling measurement (momentum or position) and so, extrapolated out, created the physical world. The many worlds interpretation postulated a near infinity of parallel worlds existed alongside our physical one, but consciousness only interacted with one or at best a few of them at a time. In fact, a mere 41 parallel universes could explain all the experiments of the quantum wave. The occasional bleed through from these other ghost universes, interworld potential, could explain UFOs, ghosts, Bigfoot, shadow spiders, you name it. It meant there could be hidden or unexplained realms within our own world. Much like

TV channels, if we weren't tuned to the right frequency, we wouldn't see them. One advantage to the MIW was that those many dimensions lurking in the background of reality could account for dark matter and dark energy, the other 95% of substance in our universe.

So, even though science was coming around to the possibility of a multidimensional reality, and the jury was still out on whether extra dimensions were provable, Daniel couldn't wait. Simply put, his experience was forcing him beyond the limits of current science. His observations, though anecdotal were *his* anecdotes and extreme, personal experience tended to trump scientific method.

Not only that, but he reasoned those dimensional barriers seemingly posed no impediment to thoughts which he knew now could be transmitted beyond the brain, so that beings, ETs and spirits, (the paranormal was very much a part of his new reality) could telepathically communicate with beings in any dimension depending upon the vibration level of the recipients. All energy vibrated, presumably at a higher rate in the higher dimensions beyond the physical universe. In the subtle energy theories of which Daniel was learning more about as his paranormal experiences grew, there were graduated levels of energy culminating in beings of pure light that vibrated at much higher rates than sluggish Earthlings.

What did this new conception mean? Daniel felt the evidence was building for a very crowded reality in the space around him, around everyone. This space could be populated with spirits, perhaps the departed, relatives and friends, but also spirit guides and guardian angels, and extraterrestrial beings, trans-dimensional entities, called watchers by some, that could exist in the interval between worlds, invisible and monitoring his – and all human - thought.

And since all was connected – *We are infinite. We are One* – were they capable of psychically controlling other, lower animals, including insects? As crazy as it sounded, Daniel had to consider it for it explained a lot of what he'd observed over the last few months.

So here were the conclusions he'd accepted. 1. Other dimensions existed that interacted with the physical world. 2. Telepathy was real with all that implied for instant universal communication. 3. If one believed that all life was truly connected, one could not be selective about which life to include or exclude. All meant ALL.

In the shamanic traditions of indigenous people worldwide, animism was certainly a well recorded phenomenon. Attribution of conscious life to all of nature, implied the potential for influence, even control, of one life form over another.

Was it such a stretch to believe that an advanced life form, an alien entity, could manifest an object from an unseen dimension into the physical world and then imbue that object, say a spider, with the faculties to interact with the life forms in the ordinary world? It could be considered a minimally invasive form of contact; Contact with an extraterrestrial race without the fear engendered by full manifestation of an ET being in its potentially frightening natural form. Might it not be a prelude to full contact with the alien species?

Many experiencers had described their ET contacts as insectoid beings. John Lennon had referred to them as cockroach-like. Some abductees called their captors spider people. In the annals of clinical DMT research, (not to mention non-clinical ayahuasca trips) the users described the other world as populated by an insect race that interacted with humans who ventured into the next dimension, and not in a negative way. They seemed to be benevolent, loving beings. Some futurists had even predicted a planetary future in which other branches of the animal kingdom, for example the insect realm, inevitably would evolve into advanced sentient beings. What could survive the nuclear destruction of Man's folly? Cockroaches, which have proven to be amazingly adaptable and enduring in the most extreme conditions.

Now he considered time: Maxine had said, and many other experiencers had echoed, the idea that time and space as we know it simply do not exist in nonphysical dimensions. That led to the inevitable conclusion that what we temporally limited Earthlings see as linear time moments must all exist together as one all-inclusive now in those dimensions. Was that what Thomas Wolf meant when he put it so succinctly in *Look Homeward Angel* – "each moment is a window on all time?" Could that mean that the future of Earth after man's destruction was in the evolution of insects? Could that mean that we are now being watched by insectoid beings from Earth's future? It was a truly a mind-boggling thought.

Daniel shook his head as if trying to shake the unwanted information out. He needed relief. He switched on the television. Perhaps a few hours of aimless "boobtubing" would clear his head of such insane thoughts. But as he surfed channels for something appealing a bizarre scene caught his eye, the climactic sequence from the science fiction movie *Midnight Special,* where the veil between reality and another dimension is briefly lifted to reveal a pristine, unpolluted landscape of futuristic architecture populated by light beings, a race of ancient watchers over humanity. With a portal thus opened, the child Alton is finally revealed to be a light entity himself and crosses over to go home. Daniel watched entranced, amazed by the synchronicity, and wondering whether the screenwriter was himself an experiencer.

In his favorite coffee shop Daniel sat with his morning coffee and an *LA Times*, when his attention was suddenly drawn to the LED TV screen overhead where Fox News was playing. There were on screen graphics of a UFO and the caption "UFOs: A New Threat to the World?" A somber male host was interviewing US Senator Thor Drummond, (R) NM.

"Senator, you've recently called for expedited public hearings on the Air Force's gun camera videos released last month showing the bizarre acrobatics of an unknown aircraft. Can you tell us what exactly your concerns are?"

"Yes, Paul, it's disconcerting to many of us in government that there are aircraft in our skies operating with total impunity. We need to know if these craft present a threat to the security of the United States. Only then can we take appropriate action."

"And what might that action be, senator?"

"It is frightening to think that we may not have the weapons to protect ourselves from any threat they may pose. Only by investigating can we determine what resources are needed to develop new technologies to defend our nation…and our world from a potential alien invasion."

"You think these craft are extraterrestrial in origin?"

"Until we study them, we just don't know. But let me remind you of what one of our greatest leaders, President Ronald Reagan, once said regarding global unity, 'I think how quickly our differences worldwide would vanish if we were facing an alien threat from outside this world.'"

Daniel picked up his phone and placed a call. "Peter, is your invitation still open?"

Chapter 19

Dusk in the high desert saw a small group of 15 or so campers draw their lawn chairs and zero gravity loungers into a circle in a remote part of Joshua Tree National Park. Daniel and Peter had just placed their chairs in an open section when Peter motioned for Daniel to come with him. "Daniel, there's someone I want you to meet." Peter led him to where a small group stood in conversation.

Peter spoke to a woman facing away from them. "Eva?" The woman turned around. She had short hair and dramatically upturned exotic eyes that swept directly to Daniel. Instantly, Daniel recognized her, the disappearing mystery woman from Contact in the Desert!

"Eva, I want you to meet my friend Daniel."

Eva extended her hand in greeting, a devilish glint in her eyes. "Hello, dear."

Daniel was briefly tongue tied but quickly found his voice. He grasped her hand, "Your lips moved." Eva grinned conspiratorially as she walked the two of them, arm in arm, back to the circle, leaving Peter rightly confused by their bizarre exchange.

The sky was dark now, lit only by starlight and a crescent moon. All looked to their leader, Eva, who sat on a mat lotus style.

(Unknown to them an Eye in the Sky surveillance satellite was monitoring them via radar technology and extreme high-resolution infrared cameras from low Earth orbit.)

Eva addressed them. "As we begin our meditation now, remember to focus on the heart/mind connection, always mindful of who we truly are, spiritual beings in a physical manifestation. Star beings yearn to connect with other children of Source. They are listening. Invite them in. Direct them here with the pure intent of love. Namaste."
The group answered "Namaste."

(The Eye in the Sky monitor screen suddenly went blank as if a cloistering veil had been dropped over the little group.)

Daniel was in deep meditation. His ghostly astral body separated from his physical body, rising into the night sky unfettered by gravity.
Astral Daniel floated above the little group, higher and higher, to overlook the night landscape washed by a weak crescent moon. Then in the blink of an eye he transitioned to a far-off location in the desert where a cacophony of voices emanated from a bunker-style building of stone on a military base. Daniel's astral body continued unabated through the heavy stone walls.
It was the Joint Security Defense Building, a sandstone-beige, ziggurat-style structure that blended into the surrounding desert hills to make it almost invisible to the naked eye from distance; it housed a secret coalition of above top-secret military units. Daniel entered at the ground level security checkpoint, floating past the unsuspecting and unseeing guards to the

elevator banks. But rather than take a car, he simply descended through the floor to the next level, where he found a barracks for staff housing.

He descended again to the next level and a long, wide corridor with high, bright lights. On either side were doors, some with small, thick plexiglass windows you could see through, others with solid, blank, metal panels. There were numbers on them but no names. All had scanners to control entry, key card, fingerprint, even retinal for the most secure. Daniel smiled at the thought of breaching such sophisticated security devices and slipped through the most secure and forbidding door.

All about were technicians quietly at work in a laboratory of some kind. Along one wall he saw rows of vats that contained embryos, human and something else, perhaps alien. This intrigued him - what sort of experimental work was happening here? He floated around the room - none of the scientists seemed able to discern his astral presence – looking over their shoulders, reading notes, trying to decipher their purpose. There were vials of material laying on the table beside the microscopes, vials labeled human skin and flesh, and alien samples, Grey, Reptilian, Mantis. In a sudden insight, whether from having just surveyed the room and its contents or perhaps having read the minds of the inhabitants of the lab with a new and amazing skill of his astral body, or both, Daniel knew their purpose was no good. A super soldier. They were seeking to create a super being for combat by combining desirable traits of the many species whose DNA was contained in the samples before them. Though the governments of all major countries had expressly outlawed it because of the dire consequences of human DNA experimentation, cloning and genetic engineering, he knew this operation must exist unknown to Congress or courts. And he knew that these beings would be birthed by unsuspecting human females, under the sophisticated military abductions program he had earlier been victimized by. MILABS – so the rumors must be true? Suddenly Daniel became nauseated; though technically had no stomach, he still felt the sensation of upchucking revulsion and had to get out of the room. With that thought, he was instantly through the floor to the next level.

One floor below, the environment was different. The lights were dim and indirect, putting most of the room in shadow. It was one large room. Along the outside walls were video consoles where drone pilots were remotely operating their craft. On the screens, operations - abduction operations? - were in progress.

Since no one reacted to his presence, Daniel still seemed to be invisible. He proceeded around the room, noting everything until he psychically bumped into a young woman soldier, a sensitive/empath, who was shocked by his sudden appearance in a secure facility; in a panic she retreated toward the center of the room. Daniel followed, floating to a large circular bank of bizarre electronic devices manned by service personnel wearing futuristic headsets that seemed to float over the cranium on a purple translucent cloud. No one was physically speaking, but the room was alive with telepathic thoughts projecting out into the ether as if from a large telephone switchboard.

A conglomeration of thoughts was heard, but with a central theme: FEAR. Fear of "others," be they black, brown, Asian, white. FEAR the police, FEAR authority, FEAR aliens, FEAR invaders from other countries, FEAR invaders from other worlds. Extraterrestrials want to conquer our planet to ENSLAVE us or EAT us. FEAR the night, aliens will snatch you out of your bed or your babies out of the womb. Nightmare images from movies, TV, books were being evoked.

In the center was an authoritative director Daniel immediately dubbed Burgundy Man, for his severe civilian look attired in a deep-red three-piece suit combo. As Daniel floated up to him, he reacted angrily to the intrusion. "You interrupt us while we're on the phones?"

"Who the hell are you?" Daniel commanded.

Then Daniel vanished. Burgundy Man barked orders. "Trace that breach! Find out who it was!"

As several people jumped into action, at a command desk on the far side of the room Daniel's trans-dimensional intrusion had not gone unnoticed by one Captain Rocco.

Daniel found himself back in his body on the desert floor in Joshua Tree National Park.

The group was awake and alert now. All eyes were on the sky where lightships were putting on a dazzling show like the one Daniel, Byron and Hoshi had witnessed in November, powering up and dashing about the sky beyond the capabilities of any conventional aircraft.

Later as the group members went around the circle sharing their experiences while in meditation, Daniel deferred when it came his turn. Eva looked directly at him. "Welcome back, Daniel." Then she addressed the group. "Daniel left us for a while." She offered no embellishment and motioned for Peter to continue sharing.

Most of the others had retired or driven into town for the night when Daniel found himself alone with Eva.

"How did you know I was gone?" he asked.

"I can bilocate in the astral during meditation. A part of me went with you."

"Where was I? What was it?"

"What do you think?"

"I sensed it was a place where bad things are done. Mind control. Abductions."

"Yes, bad things are done from your perspective but not by bad people. They think they are protecting their fellows, even you."

"I don't know if I agree with that."

"Remember, Daniel, the total number of minds in the universe is ONE. We are all connected to Source but we all journey to the truth on our own path in our own time. Source never judges, so why should we? Would you deny to others the unconditional love that you are offered and freely accept?"

Eva positioned herself directly in front of Daniel, gripped him by the shoulders and looked him straight in the eye. "Now that you've discovered their operation, Daniel, they feel threatened, and you'll be challenged. But remember this, all fear stems from fear of death. And you know now that you are not your body, that death is an illusion."

"How will it happen?"

"It will be a surprise. Three times you'll be tested, perhaps on the astral plane."

"What if I fail?"

Eva placed her left hand on Daniel's forehead and her right over his heart. Daniel's eyes closed with the quiet joy he felt in the flow of loving energy from Eva. "You won't…if you keep this connection."

When he opened his eyes, Eva was gone.

Chapter 20

Daniel arrived home from work during a lovely Fall sunset with the leaves just turning, a "frost on the pumpkin" evening. The day had been unusually warm even on the summit of Palomar Mountain, but the wind was stirring now, and the promise of seasonal change was in the air that was finally cooling after a long, hot, humid spell. The wind was up from the northwest and the trees tossed gracefully like fan dancers. Mature summer greens and aspen yellows stood out against an azure sky. The coolness and the sound of the wind in the backyard pines brought on a melancholy, a longing, and a premonition of things to come. The wind isolated Daniel, invisibly encasing his spirit in a cocoon of introspection, preparing him for the hibernation of winter to come in California's high elevations.

As ode to the passing of summer, and probably for the last time this year, he dressed casually in Bermuda shorts and flip-flops. And as the sun descended and the air temperature noticeably dropped, he determined the night would be cold and the first fireplace fire of the season was in order. The cabin was old, but when they had converted it to gas many years ago, the kitchen stove, water heater and furnace, he'd declined to run a line to the fireplace. It would have made starting a fire much easier, but he preferred to stack kindling in the firebox. It connected him to his youth-learned survival skills, scouting, and camping in the great outdoors. His one concession to modernity was the flammable fire cube, gas in solid form, that he placed at the center of his tinder construction to eliminate the wads of crumpled newspaper that were harder to come by in the digital/internet age, anyway. After neatly stacking kindling in gradually larger sizes, it was finally ready for the struck match when he realized there were no large logs in the bin. Wanting the fire to last until bedtime, as he intended to curl up before it with a good book - he hadn't yet decided between *Passport to the Cosmos* by John E. Mack, or *Kennedy's Last Stand* by Michael E. Salla – he needed fuel to replenish the little conflagration as it burned down.

Daniel's heel-slapping flip-flops clomped the few steps from the back door to the small woodshed behind the cabin, where were stacked the fruits of his and Sidd's excursion into the national forest on a firewood hunt two Falls ago.

It had been exceedingly hard work, especially for two health club conditioned scientists. Muscles developed through isolation machines like the Nautilus line did not prepare them for the arduous balancing acts of cutting and carrying logs, or wielding a chain saw over steep and uneven forest terrain. Free weights would have been better but only slightly. Lumberjacks, they had both readily conceded, deserved their manly reputation, and they vowed to never again take on such a task. For three long weekend days from dawn to dusk they had labored to twice fill Sidd's F-150 with side racks attached and estimated they'd gained about two cords of more or less uniform length logs. Now the stack in the cabin woodshed had dwindled to about half that over the last two seasons.

CHAPTER 20

In the twilight of magic hour, the afterglow of the recently set sun, Daniel could still see well enough to avoid switching on the single porcelain light fixture mounted on the wall near the front of the shed. He reached down and began quickly loading up with wood in the bend of his left arm, anxious to get back into the warmth of the cabin and strike his incendiary wand. But as he reached down with his right arm to pick up one last log, he heard a frighteningly familiar sound close at hand, a rattlesnake's warning RATTLE. To his horror in a depression of the dirt floor before him lay a timber rattler he had just uncovered, his bare ankle, foot and shin just inches away from the coiled viper, hissing and baring its poison-injecting fangs.

For a long moment Daniel was frozen in fear; If he moved, he surely would be bitten. With each passing second, his fear mounted, and the rattling intensified, as if the snake were picking up his fear. Did he take his chances and bolt quickly backwards? Would he be fast enough to get out of range of the inevitable strike the reptile would make at any quick movement? Unencumbered, maybe, but with 40 pounds of logs resting on his left arm? Not likely. Sweat oozed from his brow. A wave of bone chilling fear swept through him as he imagined the needle-like fangs striking his bare ankle, injecting poison through his bloodstream, shutting down organs and slowly killing him with its neurotoxins and hemotoxins. Simultaneously, the rattling quickened, got louder and the viper's head arched further back for attack. The rush of fear Daniel felt the snake was feeling also!

Then, in his mind's eye appeared Eva's face, calm and serene as a languid summer evening and, though her lips did not move, her voice spoke to him, reassured him, "The total number of minds in the universe is ONE."

With Eva's words, he relaxed a little, knew what to do, and while continuing to stay perfectly still, he began speaking telepathically in a soothing measured tone with clear loving intention to the snake.

"Hello, my friend. I see you've made a bed in our woodpile. Now I think you are as afraid of me as I am of you. But I don't want you to fear me anymore because I will not hurt you. You are a creation of the same Source as me. We are kin in that sense, connected by One mind."

Daniel warmed to the creature, sensing their connection in spirit. He continued. "You are beautiful, a being of perfection in your world. You have a right to life, and I will not violate that right."

It was working, the hissing had ceased, and the rattling had diminished to almost nothing. The snake's head raised higher from the coils of its body where it had been cocked to launch forward with the full force of muscle behind it. Now, though, it seemed more curious than fearful. "If you want to leave, I certainly understand as I've so rudely disturbed your sanctuary. I will not obstruct your path to freedom. Go in peace and love, my friend."

The snake's head slowly bobbed back and forth as if it were a cobra under the spell of an Indian snake charmer's pungi pipe. Then it began to slowly uncoil and cautiously probed out toward Daniel's bare foot. Daniel's body was now so hypersensitive that he felt the rattler's tiny, forked tongue on his skin like gnat wings. Satisfied that Daniel no longer posed a threat, the snake slowly moved out of the depression in the woodshed's dirt floor, crawling over Daniel's bare foot. But Daniel remained calm, felt the cool tickle of the reptile's scales on the top of his foot, closed his eyes to divert his emotions and began in a soft, breathy voice to hum a song that popped into mind, one of his favorites, "What a Wonderful World" the Louis Armstrong classic.

As the lyrics wafted through his mind he thought of nature, the azure autumn sky, rainbows, the fragile beauty of a blooming rose. And his mind calmed even more as he realized it *was* all quite wonderful, this world. And this creature before him, this animal that had engendered in him such fear for most of his life, was a part of it, a glorious part of it.

At ease at last, Daniel opened his eyes in time to watch the snake wind between his legs. He now had the full engagement of a conductor directing a familiar song, the reptile's rhythmic side-to-side undulations as mesmerizing as a wand in his hand, picking up the cadence of the music in his head.

Through the doorway and onto the lawn, the rattler disappeared in the grass at the edge of the forest.

Chapter 21

Daniel reclined in an overstuffed leather chair, feet resting on an ottoman before a roaring fire, as from out of the Echo the raspy voice of Louis Armstrong continued the song.

The living room fireplace was spectacular and what had sold them on the cabin in the first place. It covered nearly the entire wall with a wide hearth of fieldstone and cut stone mixture that continued up the wall facing. The mantle was a beautiful maple burl wood eight feet long and over a half-foot thick. The center piece on the mantle was a sprawling wrought iron candelabra with tall, slender candles bending elegantly at various odd angles, the effect of the heat from many fires below softening the wax to the inexorable effects of gravity. Though not artistically created, it could have been and would have done any artist proud. A tarnished copper lantern hung in the corner undusted with cobwebs next to a painting of 3 shawl-covered, pained women in green. "Grief" the anonymous painter had dubbed it; it had spoken to Melanie at a consignment shop in Laguna Beach, where she bought it shortly after the miscarriage.

The ordeal with the snake had emotionally exhausted Daniel; soon his body totally relaxed, and he slipped into that transition state science called hypnagogic, the waking dream. He

CHAPTER 21

had learned not to fight the paralysis that often came with it, knowing it was preparatory to OBEs for one. But also, he no longer feared these experiences as he once had with thoughts of dying or being possessed by an evil spirit and realized these were opportunities for his most lucid dreams, and, more importantly, ones he remembered in detail. This dream was no exception:

At the head of an Appalachian Mountain hollow nestled a small farmhouse among steep forested hills, poplar, beech, and oak trees, all covered with the fresh green leaves of spring. A cluster of weathered gray and unpainted outbuildings, chicken coop and barn with corral, completed the little homestead. There were livestock, a milk cow, a sow and piglets in an adjacent hog pen. White hens pecked the yard for seeds and grain while a strutting red rooster protected his harem. A covered porch ran along the full front of the modest little one-story, gable-roofed house with a spectacular view of the valley and the dirt lane that wound up the hill to the farm.

At the bottom below the house, a mountaineer man, Daniel, was turning over the grassy sod, new blades just emerging from the winter's brown matting, with a single blade plow drawn by a dark bay work horse sporting a long black mane. He briskly shouted commands: "Gee. Haw."

Up the dirt trail raced a young woman in a bonnet and calico dress who resembled Melanie, Dream Wife. She stopped at the edge of the field to briefly catch her breath before screaming across the black furrows to get her husband's attention. "Daniel! He's comin'!"

Startled, Daniel looked up from the fresh black loam furrow. "Who's comin'?"

"Devil Anse, Daniel. He's comin' for us both."

"Calm down, woman. What you talkin' about?"

"I was at Macel's just now and she heard it from the mail boy. Devil Anse said he's fed up with this fighting and feudin' and was gonna settle things with you once and for all. Daniel, they're comin' with pistols to kill us."

Daniel quickly unhitched the horse from the plow and led him toward the barn as Dream Wife ran ahead to the house. After tethering the horse and quickly tossing in a fork of hay - proper equine attending would have to wait - he hurried to the front porch where Dream Wife had fetched his lever action rifle with mounted scope. She pointed down the hollow. "I think I see'm coming up the lane."

Daniel steadied the rifle barrel against a rough-hewn oak porch column and sighted through the scope down the hollow. Through the magnified optics he saw behind the crosshairs a stern old man with two younger men beside him, determinedly striding up the lane. The old man had a no-nonsense look on his face and set the quickened pace while the youths struggled to keep up. One of the younger men carried a double barrel shotgun, the others had revolvers shoved in the waist bands of their trousers. "Yep, that's Anse and his two oldest boys," he confirmed.

Dream Wife wrung her hands, anxiously. "Oh, I knew this day was comin'. And it's three against one. Daniel, they're fixin' to kill you and rape me."

"Now don't jump to conclusions. We should hear Anse out."

"It'll be too late, then."

"You're askin' me to murder those boys?"

"Well, it's us or them."

The trio had reached a branching road intersection that led

up an adjacent run. They crossed and continued up Daniel's lane. Daniel reported, "They're comin' here alright."

"Oh, Daniel, I'm scared. The stories we've heard 'bout that man's temper. I fear we'll just be two more notches on his gun stock."

"You know, half those stories ain't true."

"Well, Clara heard that all his children are from different women, women he had his way with after he killed their husbands."

"Clara makes stuff up. You've caught her storyin' many a time."

The 3 men were getting closer and closer as they argued. Dream Wife was becoming frantic. "Daniel, you've gotta take the shot before it's too late."

In Daniel's mind were projected multiple images of dead people, mangled, bloody bodies in grotesque positions and women being violently raped, all intercut with shots of the menacing trio climbing up the hollow, getting ever closer. The intensity and pressure built with Dream Wife's incessant pleading in his ear, "Daniel, take the shot! Take the shot!" Daniel's finger put more and more pressure on the trigger as sweat beaded on his brow and trickled down his sun reddened cheeks. The crescendo built to a confusing cacophony of noise and violent images that overloaded his senses.

Sensing his weakness, Dream Wife screamed her ultimatum, "If you LOVE ME, Daniel, take the shot!"

In response, Daniel bellowed a long, piercing, primal scream and threw the gun down. "NOOOO! I will not kill out of fear! Fear of what MIGHT happen!"

Immediately, the scene changed, Dream Wife was gone, and Daniel was alone on the porch, with the trio standing in the yard before him, smiling broadly, their weapons nowhere to be seen. Anse spoke cheerfully. "Daniel, my brother, I've come to make peace."

Chapter 22

Daniel awakened with a start. The fire had burned down to embers leaving the living room in almost complete darkness. He pondered the lucid dream; its scenes and emotions vivid and fresh as if he had experienced it physically in real time. Often, such threshold experiences left him questioning reality and this one especially so. Had he been to another dimension? An alternate universe? He remembered the smells and textures of that realm, the fecund aroma of freshly turned soil, the manure stench of the barn and the masking smell of the hay, felt the rough grain of the oak post on his calloused fingers. What did it mean? It had seemed like a test, and one he had passed. A test of how far fear would propel his actions, to the point of killing? But a test by whom? In the middle of this internal questioning, he heard a metallic knock in the dark shadow to the far left of the fireplace.

"Who's there?" he called to the blackness.

Silence. Daniel had become used to house noises in the cabin, various sounds that he had gradually learned to connect to his thoughts, strange as that was to accept. But eventually he just had to conclude from the timing alone that entities - spirits, ghosts, ETs perhaps - hid in the ether all around him, invisible, monitoring his movements…and, yes, his thoughts.

Such paranoid thinking would have sent him to a shrink for most of his adult life up until that fateful night in the desert. In one historic 12-hour period, his concept of the possible had changed forever.

But this sound was different. This Daniel knew was connected to a real physical being. He continued, louder, "I know someone is there. I command you. Reveal yourself."

From the deep shadow he heard an animal grunt, then a figure stepped forth to reveal a large and menacing silhouette backlit by the soft moonlight from the front bow window. To better see, Daniel switched on the crackle-glass table lamp beside him and gasped when the light revealed a 7-foot-tall, green-scaled, reptilian humanoid in archaic battle armor. The fearsome alien carried a long hammer-like weapon with a double axe head, and crouched into a combat stance, teeth bared, and uttered a challenging guttural growl.

Once again Daniel confronted the face of fear. He leaped out of the easy chair and backed off, wisely fleeing from this new danger.

The reptilian warrior started forward swinging the battle axe in a wide arc before him, effortlessly sliced through the trunk of a well-matured Ficus tree, then with his large, muscled leg easily kicked the heavy ceramic pot aside. It cracked apart scattering its root bound soil on the oak hardwood floor. Clearly, this was no dream or hallucination. Deftly using his thick muscled tail like a *T. Rex*, as a fifth appendage in coordination with his other limbs, the amphibian being easily flung couch, chairs, and tables aside, pulverizing knickknacks and the crackle-glass lamp under his crushing weight, as he cleared a wide path to his vulnerable quarry. Objects flew at Daniel like projectiles from a catapult, or an air cannon, as

CHAPTER 22

he back away from the onslaught. Something hard impacted his forehead, and he lost his balance, stumbled into an end table, and fell hard. As he scrambled away on all fours, he frantically searched for a weapon, something to use as a club, knife, anything, but there was nothing. As he bumped against the living room/kitchen dividing wall, he looked to his right for the kitchen archway and possible escape out the back door, but it was blocked by the same easy chair he had been sleeping in just a few minutes ago.

He was trapped in his own home; a domestic sanctuary it was no more. And now something warm and familiar trickled down his nose and into his mouth. Blood, his own blood. He recalled the salty taste from his childhood injuries, but then it had been a split lip at most. Now he feared he was facing worse, much worse.

He was unarmed against a fierce, aggressive, warrior intent on his subjugation or…death. And completely helpless…or was he?

In Daniel's mind flashed the image of Eva's hands, one resting on his head, the other on his heart and he heard again her words. "Keep the connection." As he struggled to stand again, a completely new thought dawned in Daniel consciousness, causing him to pause, suspending his fear. Remembering Eva, it was as if a veil had been lifted from his perception. The flow of time slowed; the violent action he witnessed in his field of vision now seemed choreographed by an unseen conductor, a complex symphony of force vectors as the objects arced, collided and fell with a beautiful grace, as if they were playing out in a slow-motion movie scene. He saw clearly at once; the whole of the moment which was infinite, and the truth was there, so easy, so right. Instead of retreating further, or cowering before his attacker to plead for mercy, he stopped, stood tall and calmly addressed the beast. "Hello, captain."

Daniel's words slammed into the reptile like a force repellent; he abruptly halted his assault and he too straightened up to full height, 7 feet of armor-clad muscle, slitted yellow eyes glaring down at the puny, fragile, and bleeding, human before him.

After a long stare down in which Daniel did not blink, the reptilian warrior visibly exhaled, and then morphed into the quite human Captain Rocco, clad in his Air Force uniform. He addressed Daniel in a calm, matter-of-fact tone, "Professor."

Daniel replied with admirable aplomb. "That was impressive."

"But not convincing." It was not a question.

"Oh, it was. Except I had help." He smiled at the thought. "Her name is Eva."

The captain conceded this with an understanding grimace. Then surprised Daniel with his next words: "We've met."

He accepted the admission, and its revealing connotation; he was learning not to question the interwoven tentacles of the new reality he was now living. Sensing a new and deeper connection to the transmogrified human before him, he probed. "Tell me, Captain, what's it like to shape shift between species?"

Now Captain Rocco was genuinely surprised. "No human has ever asked me that." Then he smiled wryly, remembering. "The first time I morphed to human, I didn't know what to do with all the emotions. Very confusing."

"We are a complex species."

"And I missed my tail. Still do. Sometimes I lose my balance."

Realizing Rocco was admitting to a human-like vulnerability, Daniel nodded his appreciation. Later he would marvel at how

CHAPTER 22

quickly the situation had normalized. But it was time to get down to the nitty gritty. "Was the snake yours?"

With a slight bob of the head, the captain conceded this. "Well, done…Daniel."

"And the dream?"

Captain Rocco repeated the gesture.

Daniel sighed, his body sagged against the wall, fatigue finally setting in. "When will it end?" he lamented.

Rocco's eyes squinted as his mind registered the guileless nature of the extraordinary being before him, who had no inkling of what he had just accomplished. "It just did."

"I'm safe?"

"We don't harm people with your…enlightenment."

For a long moment Daniel was at a loss for words; then, as he surveyed the shambles of his living room, his eyes fell on the broken ceramic pot with it's severed trunk stump, and he realized the irony. "That Ficus tree was pretty ignorant."

Captain Rocco shrugged while uttering a low hiss, what amounted to a reptilian chuckle, before agreeing. "A real knot head."

Chapter 23

So stoked was his energy from the encounters, Daniel was awake much of the night. Captain Rocco had stayed around to help him clean up, at least move things back in the living room to make some order again, to enable him to get around. He had asked Daniel if it were all right to morph back into his reptilian self. "I'm much stronger and this will go quicker," he reasoned, then added, "I'll lose the armor."

At first Daniel had hesitated from residual fear, and PTSD of the incident, but assented. He was grateful then for the experience. As he watched Rocco, now reptilian, work, he quickly got over the initial fear of seeing him transformed again and was instead filled with admiration. Reptilian Rocco was a physically beautiful being. His skin was an deeply rich emerald green, his scales amazingly complex and iridescent, each graduated in subtle hues. His heavily muscled body had the definition of a champion body builder, 7-foot, 400-pound Arnold Schwarzenegger, and he performed with a dexterity and grace that was nothing short of balletic.

When cleanup was finished and he, as Captain Rocco again, bid him adieu, Daniel was curious. "How did you get here?" He would not have been surprised if Rocco had said his personal flying saucer was idling on the roof. But the captain had surprised him once again. "My SUV is parked just down the road."

"You drove here?" He said, a little too incredulously.

"Yeah, my broomstick was in the shop." Rocco replied.

Daniel guffawed, head back and unrestrained. Were they becoming friends? When he'd composed himself once again, he inquired, "Are you also on the Air Force quidditch team?"

With a head nod, he answered, "Goalie. Tail comes in handy."

"I can imagine." Daniel marveled at the thought, then added more seriously, "Do you drive to all your…tests?"

"Only when I work locally."

When he finally did get to bed, Daniel immediately felt his exhaustion and soon dropped off into a deep sleep. But ironically, this night of extraordinary events was not yet over. Daniel's astral being slipped out of his physical body and rose through the roof into the atmosphere. This time without hesitation he headed for high Earth orbit, his blue marble home world glowing far below, into an immense mother ship that manifested as if anticipating him. Inside was a grand room with a high vaulted cathedral ceiling and granite columns that opened to a terrace with 3-tiered water fountain and a stunning view. From the ship's high vantage, a rugged desert landscape stretched hundreds of miles toward a distant horizon under a pinkish blue sky. The vast canyon was reminiscent of, but was not, the Grand Canyon. The reddish color was most likely due to rusted iron minerals in the soil, he reasoned, observing a dust devil snake its way across the arid landscape. It must be an alien world and he couldn't take his curious eyes from it until he saw Eva approaching. She radiated an ethereal glow, resplendent in a pearly white, full-length, iridescent robe that flowed in her wake as she strode toward Daniel, looking far less regal in his pajama bottoms. Her slanting eyes were literally alive with joy as she greeted him with an embrace, heart to heart.

After drinking long of her loving essence, he asked, "Eva, is this your home?"

"One of them. On this plane we can manifest what we want. On this momentous occasion I thought this look appropriate."

He motioned to the landscape. "What is this place?"

"You don't recognize it?"

He looked harder, searching for familiar detail. "It's not Earth?"

She shook her head while waving her arm to indicate he should look to the horizon. In the distance he saw one large wispy cloud-capped mountain that dominated. There were no other mountains visible and even from this distance the caldera was obvious, "Olympus Mons?" He screamed. "Mars!"

Eva laughed.

He drank in the sights trying to soak up detail of this astronomer's dream come true, floating somewhere above the surface of the Red Planet, staring at the largest volcano in the solar system, 72,000 feet, two and one-half times the height of Mt. Everest.

"Then this is Valles Marineris." He referred to the Red Planet's immense canyon, longer, wider, and deeper than Earth's Grand Canyon.

Daniel James, PhD, witnessed a sight no human had seen, not even remotely through the many Martian rovers from the Seventies *Sojourner* to 2021's *Ingenuity*.

With a million questions filling his mind, he was about to ask his first when Eva, firmly grasping Daniel by the arm, pulled him away from the panorama and led him away to an alcove where they sat by a marble fireplace and a roaring fire that, though real in 3D sight and sound, radiated no heat. When he was about to protest, she cut him off with a stern, parental shake of the head. "How are you faring from your tests?"

"Tests? They felt more like ordeals."

"They might have felt like attacks, but they were really gifts."

"Gifts?"

"You were being shown your fears, so face-to-face you could vanquish them, and become stronger, self-empowered."

"How was it helping me to face such a traumatic experience? When he started his attack, I was sure he meant to kill me."

"If he hadn't been convincing you wouldn't have learned anything because there would not have been enough at stake. Fear of death focuses one. Tell me, Daniel, what do you think you learned? Take them one at a time. The rattlesnake?"

"I remembered your words, 'The total number of minds in the universe is One.' We are brothers in spirit, the reptile and me, connected."

"And the dream?"

He pondered momentarily, "I think I was tested to see just how far fear, irrational fear, would drive me. To murder innocent people over a misunderstanding?"

"The reptilian attack."

"This is the toughest to figure out. But with your help I kept my head-heart connection and was able to relax, think clearly and allow the truth to reveal itself. When I saw who the reptilian alien was behind the mask, I knew I was in control."

"Excellent, Daniel."

"What I don't really understand is why Rocco didn't kill me anyway. If he'd ignored me, I was still at his mercy, and he could have still accomplished his goal."

"So, what was his goal?" Daniel shook his head in resignation. "Daniel, there are beings in this universe that can seem evil, but they are only foils, playing a role for our soul development. When we come into physical three-dimensional reality, we enter a realm of duality. It seems contradictory but duality, yin/yang, good/bad, exists for the sake of teaching Unity consciousness. XiLinq, Captain Rocco's reptilian name, is one such being. Reptilians of his race work with the service-to-self forces in the government because that is what those forces want. Their consciousness of selfishness invited Rocco's race in because their thoughts manifested it. It does not make XiLinq and his fellow beings evil. Rest assured XiLinq does not consider what he does evil, but a necessary service to Source and therefore to us all."

"Why did he stop his attack?"

"Because he knew you knew. You had grown in spirit enough to get past the immediate fear to the truth. He had done his job, whether he was fully aware of it or not."

"He said I'm safe now because they don't harm enlightened people."

"What better proof that he was only playing a role?"

"I see the value of understanding life from a broad perspective, but I guess I don't know how enlightenment could protect, say…stop a bullet."

"What if the bullet is never fired?" Her gaze pierced him to the soul. "With enlightenment comes love, and all love begins with self-love. A being that can't love itself cannot love others."

"I've heard that but never understood it. There seem to be many people that serve others yet are full of self-loathing. It would seem their good deeds are a compensation for low self-esteem."

"Let me put it this way. If you agree that all life in the universe is One, then how can you hate any one being, especially yourself, and not have it affect all other life? By loving yourself you by default must love all others for we are all connected. It doesn't mean we must be passive. We can dislike what people do and still love them. A mother might abhor her children's behavior but never stops loving them."

"But how is love powerful? It seems the opposite of strength in many ways."

"Love can be characterized by those who go to great lengths to portray it as weak. The woolly thinking, bleeding heart liberal? They do this out of fear for love's power."

Daniel pondered this. "Am I enlightened?"

"How do you feel?"

"I don't feel different."

"You are on the path." When he appeared unconvinced, she added, "There was a monk who became enlightened. When asked how he felt, the monk replied, 'As miserable as before.' Enlightenment is not a destination, Daniel, but a journey."

With that Daniel was transported back to his bedroom in the cabin where he awoke with a start. After asking Alexa to switch on the bedside lamp, he reached for pen and notebook and began recording his dream.

Chapter 24

In the Palomar Mountain Observatory offices Daniel and Sidd walked in the corridor side by side toward Director Sauer's office. As they approached his closed door, they heard indistinct but raised voices from inside, so they waited without knocking. Sidd worried, "Wonder what this is all about?"

"Maybe we're getting the axe," Daniel offered.

"Don't joke about that. I have a family; I can't be on the job market again."

"Sidd, don't worry," Daniel said, reassuringly, before adding a little sarcasm. "Besides, aren't you *der fuehrer's* darling now?"

Understanding immediately where Daniel's resentment was coming from, Sidd offered a defense. "Danny, I wanted you on the project with me. I don't know why I didn't insist on it from the beginning. But I will, I just haven't had a chance to bring it up to Sauer, yet." He paused and took a deep breath before continuing. He had thought a lot about this moment and finally went there. "And that 2-ton elephant? I've never said a thing to anyone, not even Deepa." He paused again before attempting a little levity. "Well, I did tell my sweet Kamala while rocking her to sleep one night. But she can keep a secret."

Daniel smiled, appreciating Sidd's irrepressible humor even in apology, perhaps especially in apology. "Hey, it's good to unburden to someone. I'm glad she knows."

"You know, you are like a brother, and I love you," Sidd was unusually emotional today, it seemed.

"I know, buddy. We were both going through stuff. It'll all work out."

The voices had come closer now. As the door opened, they saw Dr. Sauer and Dr. Bains standing inside. Bains took Daniel by the elbow. "Daniel. Walk with me."

Dr. Sauer curtly motioned for Sidd to come inside.

Outside Daniel and Dr. Bains talked as they strolled up the meandering footpath toward the Hale Building on the campus grounds. "I had a conversation with Dr. Sauer just now."

"We heard. I mean, not the content, but the…emotion."

"Dr. Sauer has decided to retire this year," he offered quickly, and without waiting for a response added, "I was just encouraging it."

"And he didn't take it well?"

"Sauer is old school; his mentor was Donald Menzel."

"Dr. Menzel, the debunker?"

"You know of him?" His tone betrayed a little surprise.

"I read his books. He was instrumental in forming my first opinions of UFOs."

Donald Howard Menzel was one of the first theoretical astronomers in the United States. As a popular author he had written the first edition of *A Field Guide to the Stars and Planets* the year before he died in 1976. But many people already knew him from 3 books he wrote debunking UFOs including *Flying Saucers – Myth – Truth – History* and *The UFO Enigma*, both of which Daniel had read while yet in high school but had already set his sights on a career in astronomy. Menzel was one of the highest academic authorities on the subject and the thesis of all his popular books was "UFOs are all misidentified natural phenomena." That had also been Daniel's personal and professional position...up until Joshua Tree.

"Did you know he was one of the original Majestic 12?"

"One of you guys?"

"A pioneer, you might say."

"I can't really say I'm surprised anymore."

"Dr. Menzel's books were meant to throw cold water on the theories in books of government authorities like Ruppelt and Keyhoe."

Bains referred to Edward J. Ruppelt, the former head of the Air Force's Project Blue Book, who wrote a classic in the field of ufology, *The Report on Unidentified Flying Objects* in 1956 after he had left the program. Donald Keyhoe, on the other hand was a retired Marine Corps pilot, who wrote a Fifties book, *The Flying Saucers Are Real,* and became the first popular authority on the subject. He claimed to know that the Air Force considered UFOs extraterrestrial and were conducting an elaborate cover up. Early on, Keyhoe called for the government to release all their files. Daniel, while aware of books like those of Ruppelt and Keyhoe, nonetheless considered them little more than extensions of popular mass market rags that catered to the wishful imaginings of the "great uneducated" and refused to read them, preferring what he considered the scientific reasoning of Menzel's books.

Menzel's connection to the early cover up was new to Daniel, but his surprise at reality being turned upside down was less and less with each revelation. The Majestic 12 referred to the reported first committee formed in 1947, shortly after the Roswell crash, of military and science professionals tasked by President Truman with managing the cover up. Prominent

CHAPTER 24

names of members were Gen. Hoyt Vandenberg, former Air Force Chief of Staff and former Director of the CIA; Vannevar Bush, who oversaw the Manhattan Project and became the first presidential science advisor; and James Forrestal, former Secretary of the Navy and the first Secretary of Defense. Daniel was aware of the name Majestic 12 but knew little about it, preferring to believe the reports that the FBI had declared the original documents revealing the list of members to be fake. This new information that one of his science heroes was a founding member meant once again he did not know the full story.

"Are you forcing Dr. Sauer out?"

"The day of those like him is past; modern diplomacy requires finessing skills that are just beyond their comprehension." He took a moment before adding, "Daniel, you'll be stepping into his shoes."

"Me? Why?"

"I told you with the right decisions your career could be greatly advanced."

Nonplussed by this unexpected news, Daniel could only shake his head in dismay. "I figured you were here to fire me."

"On the contrary, we still want you on board Astralis, though your role will change."

"But I can't be your authoritative debunker," he countered, still not quite believing Bains.

"It's not expected."

"Ben, I still need to know more about the culture I'll be working in. You said at another time you'd explain about your early involvement in gravity research and the article from 1952 that credited you with discovering gravity particles."

Baines studied him, and realized he was serious. "All right, let's find a private place to talk."

Daniel led him to a quiet little grotto where they were shielded from the public areas of the campus by rocks, pine trees and laurel shrubs; there were benches for people to sit on and meditate or just relax in nature. A fountain bubbled with running water to provide a mask to intruding outside noise. It was rarely used and in fact many people who worked at the complex didn't even know of its existence - the perfect place for a private conversation.

After they had settled in on adjacent benches so they could converse in normal tones, Bains began. "The article you read was right, for the most part. My partner and I did make some important discoveries about gravity. But we subsequently learned a lot more once the project went dark."

"So antigravity is real?"

"Oh yes. But we didn't need our research to learn that. We had ships to study."

"The downed ship from Roswell?"

"That and others. The first crash and retrieval of an ET craft was in Italy in 1933. Mussolini got that one. Our first was 1941 in Cape Girardeau, Missouri, and in 1942, after the Battle of Los Angeles, when the Navy recovered drones shot down offshore. And then the Haunebu German craft that came with Project Paperclip, like the one you saw at the Chocolate Mountain facility."

"Yes, the saucer with swastikas on it! So, you knew about my abduction?"

"An unfortunate misunderstanding. Colonel McDonald is sometimes overzealous with his recruiting techniques."

"So, with Nazi technology and back engineering of downed ET craft, you were successful in developing G-engines after

CHAPTER 24

all?"

"Don't forget the early electro-gravitics work of Townsend Brown and Nikola Tesla."

"I've seen the names. So, our military has developed working prototypes of antigravity spacecraft?"

Bains smiled at his charge's naivete, then said matter-of-factly. "We have fleets of ships in operation, space flotillas."

Daniel's wide-eyed, jaw-dropped stare told Bains he had no idea of the level of technological achievement of black operations. "Daniel, we have been secretly developing this technology for over 70 years now. You might say we've been quite successful."

"What do you mean by a flotilla? Literally a fleet of warships like a naval armada?"

"Exactly, only traveling space, not the seas of Terra."

"But how is it possible to keep this secret? Where are these craft?"

"Deployed to the stars. There are two separate operations, one by the Air Force and another operated by the Navy." He paused, "You could say three, I guess, if you count the Space Force of Trump, who by the way has no idea of our operations. In fact, few presidents have had such knowledge since Reagan. Bush 41 kept it from Carter; Clinton did find out about it through Lawrence Rockefeller but was 'persuaded' not to go public. Bush 43 was read in partially, and Obama, well, you could say he was a "product" of the program."

Off Daniel's bemused look, Bains shook his head, "A conversation for another time. It's a lot to take in at one sitting."

"Does this mean we've had manned missions in the solar system?"

"Much more. We have permanent bases on the far side of

the moon, Mars, Titan, Europa. And have had deep space expeditions to other stars, by ourselves and with help of certain ET civilizations. The 'exchange program' at the end of the *Close Encounters* movie was based on fact."

"But how has it been possible to keep this secret?"

"The cover up started in earnest after Roswell. After the base commander sent out his press release to the world, the cat was out of the bag. Remember the American psyche was fragile at that time. On one hand our military men were invincible heroes, had defeated the Nazis *and* the Imperial forces of Japan. How would the public have accepted the truth that our world was now confronted with an 'enemy' so far advanced that our cutting-edge weaponry, even A-bombs, were useless against them?"

"I'm guessing not well."

"America and the world needed a rest, respite from the world wars we'd endured. It was how so many Nazis and their vast stolen wealth were able to escape and disappear into Western society…and corporations. No one had the stomach for continuing hostilities in any form. That's why, symbolically, Hitler's reported death was so important. It meant closure for the world."

"Reported? I didn't know it was in question?"

"Another tale for another time. Let's just say Bormann and Hitler had more than a year to plan their exit; they knew the war was lost long before the Allies received Germany's surrender."

Daniel was overwhelmed. On the one hand he was not surprised that we'd developed technology to travel space far beyond chemical rockets, he'd seen firsthand what was possible that night in the desert as the immense mother ship rose silently into the sky over Joshua Tree. So, he could not doubt the science that made it possible; but the extent to which it had been developed? He just was not prepared for Dr. Bains's revelations. Earth humans had conquered space and colonized the solar system! The dreams of his youth were real and no one, but a select few, knew it. He wanted more answers now and Bains seemed to have them.

"What about George Adamski? In a sense he pulled me into all this. The guys in the desert that night were only there because of him. Yet, he was both adored and reviled. So much of what he claimed about his Venusian space brothers is now known to be fiction. But now that I know what I know, I don't think he was the fraud so many consider him."

"The Fifties contactees are interesting cases. Adamski did make contact, but with Germans masquerading as alien beings. That's why the information he received is dated now. It was meant for the masses based on what the public, through astronomers not unlike yourself, knew at the time, or more accurately what was speculated about our solar system.

"Even prior to WWII, Germany had been establishing extensive bases in Antarctica, mostly under the ice. It was where their post war successful saucer technology escaped to, leaving to the Allies the failed experiments, craft like the early Haunebu you saw. The American military knew of this base and considered it a threat, so Truman launched a task force led by Admiral Byrd, Operation High Jump to the public, that was ostensibly a scientific expedition. But the real, and secret, objective was to capture or neutralize the Nazi forces established there. The six-month expedition was back in a few weeks with excuses, but the real reason was they were thoroughly defeated by the weaponized saucers they encountered. Admiral Byrd as much as admitted this publicly when he warned that the next war would come when the United States was attacked by craft coming from the Poles."

"He wasn't speaking hypothetically," interjected Daniel. "Like Reagan in his warning about aliens attacking Earth?"

"Many people assume that now. But no, he meant it literally from what he'd witnessed in Antarctica. Further proof of this deadly Nazi force came in 1952 with the famous Washington, DC, fly over. You've probably seen the photos of that."

"Yes, I guess I assumed they must have been faked somehow."

"No fake. It was a warning to our government that they sign a treaty with the so-called Nazi Antarctic Break Away Civilization. In 1955, Ike signed."

Bains watched Daniel as he mentally grappled with the information. He knew but for Daniel's ET encounter experiences, Daniel might have dismissed Bains as just another conspiracy theory crackpot. Time for some stroking of the ego. He rose and motioned for Daniel to follow him. As they walked down the public path toward the parking lot, he spoke encouragingly, "Daniel, you've impressed some rather powerful people. Especially XiLinq."

"You know him?"

"Oh yes. He met with Dr. Hynek and me. Daniel, the world we live in is complex enough. You add in off-world civilizations, and the problems increase exponentially. Not all of us in service to Earth agree with everything the military does. But we understand that for better or worse, warriors need enemies. And civilians need protecting. But we also need enlightened teachers. That's what you can be, a spiritual warrior if you will."

"I'm not sure that metaphor works."

CHAPTER 24

"Then make up your own. The point is that we're more or less muddling our way through this exo-politics business." He paused, wondering if he should go on, then did. "Daniel, the Majestic-12 charter, actually the MJ stood for Mars-Jupiter, was revised in 1987 under an ultra-top-secret order by President Ronald Reagan. The Director of the NSA became Chairman, and all elected officials had to be voted in by majority of the permanent members. And that included any sitting POTUS after Reagan. Being president did not automatically get you in. And furthermore, NO spiritual or religious leaders were allowed membership." Bains paused again to let that sink in. "We now think it was a mistake to exclude spiritually developed people. Religious leaders and their fundamentalist dogmas will still be barred, but we know alien contact has an important spiritual component. Someone with your metaphysical abilities can help us in diplomacy with ET beings, so that the generals don't always see everything as a nail that needs hammering with a ballistic missile or a laser cannon."

"I don't have any answers. I seem to be muddling along…on a different path. I'm just learning the immense power of love, corny as that sounds. And the interconnection of all things. Someone once told me I would learn that I was not alone in every sense of the word. I realize now she meant there is no privacy even in our thoughts."

"That's an unsettling thought…to many."

"But a very empowering one. Once enough people realize no one gets by with anything, ever, then the world will be a better place. No man is an island was never truer."

They had reached the parking lot and Bains's car, a black SUV with black out window tinting. Bains climbed in but before closing the door, he added one final caveat. "FYI only right now. Wait for Sauer's announcement before telling anyone." With that he drove off, leaving Daniel alone to silently consider his unexpected good fortune.

Chapter 25

The cabin living room was in order again, minus knickknacks, glass-framed pictures and small decorative items destroyed in XiLinq's assault; the furniture had mostly survived, if the Ficus had not. Once again Daniel was curled up before a crackling fire with a book, this time Michael E. Salla's *US Air Force Secret Space Program*.

If Salla's reporting could be believed, Dr. Bains had been right about the dark ops world's development of a clandestine space fleet. Not only that, but the author claimed that there were 4 such space programs emanating from Earth, the afore mentioned Air Force and Navy programs, and the Nazi Antarctic force, plus the alien Nordic space command fleet. One bit of confirmed evidence had impressed Daniel, though: the hidden-in-plain-sight anti-gravity technology of the B-2 Stealth bomber. Experts who evaluated the openly acknowledged Spirit bomber claimed its conventional engines were radically under powered for the craft's published weight. This, they contended, was evidence that electro-gravitics were incorporated in its design, specifically on the leading edge of the flying wing. Townsend Brown's patented design for electro-gravitics reduced weight and if the Spirit's *operational* weight were far less than its static weight, the smaller engines' reduced thrust could push the B-2 to Mach 1.5, (1.5 times the speed of sound), or more. Daniel reasoned that if the military was willing to divulge this technologically sophisticated craft, though still rudimentary by UFO standards, what were they *not* revealing to us? Seventy years, as Bains had said, was a long time to develop known science. The rumored Aurora program with its SR-74 and SR-75, reportedly capable of up to Mach 24 beyond the threshold of space - 16,000 MPH! - was staggering to imagine.

An interstellar flotilla of spacecraft, Bains had said. The idea excited Daniel. And with that he retired to the bedroom to dream of voyaging to Mars, Jupiter, and star systems beyond.

In a very dark room Daniel slept soundly when a loud knock rudely awakened him. Greatly irritated, he shouted into the darkness, "Now what?"

Silence was his answer. Then, as he lay quietly watching, senses on high alert, a golden orb slipped through the outer wall into the room as if the logs were not even there. It hovered over Daniel, bathing him in a golden glow. There was no need to say anything; he immediately felt the connection. When the orb moved out through the bedroom door and down the hall, Daniel obediently followed it.

Outside the orb flew through the front door, over the porch and into the yard. The door opened and Daniel followed it out, off the porch and onto the grass. He was only wearing a pajama bottom in the cool moonless night air. The orb, moving quickly, disappeared into an odd green foggy mist that had settled at the trees edge.

Daniel continued up to the mist but hesitated to go further. He saw movement inside, a flash of fur; it was an animal. As he waited the animal moved forward and came to the edge of the mist, but in the dim light he could not quite make it out. Hesitantly, he spoke to the being or whatever it was. "I know somebody's there. Come forward so I can see you."

The creature moved forward, and he saw a familiar canine nose. For a moment Daniel could not believe his own eyes. "Jesse?" The dog edged out farther, and he saw that it was indeed Jesse. The tears filling his eyes nearly blinded him and his throat choked the words as he tried to speak. Finally, he was able to call softly, "Oh, Jesse, Jesse. Is it you, my baby? Come here."

Jesse, cautiously, came closer as Daniel, half disbelieving, put forth a tentative hand to touch him. When his hand felt solid flesh, Daniel let out a spontaneous cry of joy. "You're real!"

Jesse came close enough so Daniel, now down on his knees, could fully embrace him. Pet and master were in full love feast now, renewing their relationship. After several minutes Daniel stood and motioned for Jesse to follow him into the house. "Come on boy, let's get you home. I'll call Melanie and then we'll drive into town. She'll be over the moon. Just like me." But Jesse held back. Daniel stopped and turned back. "What's wrong, Jess?"

Jesse walked back to the green mist, clearly meaning for Daniel to follow. Jesse stopped at the edge of the forest where the green mist began and waited. Another figure could be seen moving in the dim light. Daniel watched as a small child stepped forward. Jesse licked his cheek tenderly and softly whimpered. The child was about 4 years old, slight of build, and frail. He was wearing a one-piece jump suit of metallic gray color. A crop of wispy gold hair fell on an oversize forehead with large blue eyes that had a distant, vacant look. Though there was an unmistakable androgyny in the child, Daniel believed he was male.

Jesse nuzzled the child forward, wanting Daniel to meet him. Daniel fell to his knees again in front of the child as slowly his eyes widened, and he experienced unmistakable recognition. He began to weep again, silently, tears running down his cheeks. He gently touched the fragile little being before him, knowing they were connected somehow. Bewildered, the child stared inquisitively and reached out to briefly touch Daniel's tears, as if he had never seen them before. Daniel gently hugged the boy, sobbing now.

Confusion washed over the child's face; affection was a new experience. For the first time in his brief life, he was the recipient of human emotional attachment, an object of affection. He felt it in the tactile warmth of the body entwined around his own, and more, in the absorption of subtle energy in his chakras, even through their garments, in his flesh and skin that touched the human male. And just as importantly he absorbed the man's energy in his head, felt a melding of their minds. The man's essence, his spirit, touched a virgin, naked spot in the child's soul. With this spirit came memories, experiences of human intimacy, of a man and a woman, this man and a human woman, a female who was somehow familiar to the child, also. The child could feel what they felt in another moment of closeness, could feel what their bodies had felt in that moment, the roughness of a fibrous substance against their skin, the cool wind on bare flesh, the mingled smell of pleasant aromas – of he knew not what - the tensing of muscles as the electricity of a pleasurable fire coursed through them. He felt too the joyful light of Source that passed between them, which he recognized, for he was of the same Source, felt the anchors weighing their emotions break free, felt the peace and fulfillment of creation, HIS creation. And in that moment as all was absorbed into his being; he welcomed it as one accepts a precious gift. From vacant bewilderment to comprehension, his eyes mirrored his awakened soul as human DNA memory kicked in. For the first time he felt the inexplicable emotional experience that is…love. His head fell on Daniel's shoulder, tiny arms completed their embrace and from his great blue eyes flowed virgin tears.

In the midst of this emotional event the 3 figures were suddenly bathed in an intense beam of white light from directly overhead where a large ship hovered just over the trees. The light revealed other beings in the clearing, 3 small Greys and a tall Mantis being. The Mantis being stepped forward as the Greys escorted Jesse and the child back toward the green mist. His voice projected into Daniel's mind telepathically. "You have done well, Daniel. You've activated his emotional faculties. But the boy is not yet ready for human society."

"He is my child?" Daniel didn't quite believe he was asking that question, but he knew he must.

"Do not think in terms of ownership. He was made with three different DNA strands."

"Three?"

"Yes, yours, Melanie's and ours."

"Melanie is his mother?"

"Yes, he was taken from her after the first trimester."

"Her miscarriage!"

"Rather a necessary procedure. He would not have survived a human birth."

"But if he can't live on Earth, how will we ever know him?"

"You have done tonight more than you can imagine. He will

continue to develop with us until it is hoped one day he can survive in your world."

"He'll live on your ship."

"Ours and many others. He is a child of the stars."

"If he can't stay here, how will I convince Melanie?"

"She already knows. We are visiting her, also."

"Now? But how?"

"Time is not as you perceive it."

As Daniel turned again to the mist, the child was there awaiting his glance and grinned beatifically. An unmistakable light had turned on in his eyes. Jesse stood beside him. "And Jesse?"

"His work is done now."

"But we love him so. If we can't have our son, why not him?"

"He too is not as you think."

As Daniel watched, Jesse transformed into a beautiful golden light orb. "This soul has other work to do."

Daniel smiled once more at the child and he smiled back. Then, he and the orb disappeared into the mist, and the light beam flashed off.

But the darkness that followed was only momentary as another light glowed from behind Daniel. He turned to see standing in the dark clearing none other than a radiant Hoshi clad in the same gleaming white raiment as on the mother ship. As Daniel watched, Hoshi extended a hand and invited another being from the shadow into his light. Daniel gasped as it was Melanie; their eyes locked in loving connection filled with a calm serenity that revealed that she had had her own revelation. Both figures were transparent, not present in their physical bodies, but their astral representation. Then too that light faded out and Daniel was left standing alone in the clearing.

CHAPTER 25

He looked up at the large ship hovering over the cabin just before it also flashed out and the sky was empty except for stars, stars, stars.

Daniel had just pulled into the driveway. As he climbed out of his Polestar and walked up to the front door, Melanie was waiting at the foyer just inside. From the Echo in the adjacent living room came the raspy voice of Louis Armstrong singing "What a Wonderful World".

The two embraced - "heart to heart" - like long parted lovers and, although nothing was spoken, each understood that their lives had been changed forever.

Epilogue

And the StarChild, union of Mother Earth and Father Sky, taught the People to live from their hearts.

Two years later in the Greenway Visitor center, a lecture was in progress given by Daniel. His name tag read Director of Observatories.

"So as Webb and THEIA continue to search the heavens for livable planetary atmospheres, one day soon we may just find proof in the sky of extraterrestrial life." He paused for polite applause. "Now are there any questions?"

A hand rose in the crowd, but Daniel could not see who it was.

"Yes, in the back."

"What do you think of the hypothesis that we have been visited by alien races all through our history?" The voice was male and youthful with a high pitch but spoke perfectly articulated English, slightly monotone, as a very high-end AI might speak.

"Good question. I think our universe is so vast and complex that to believe we are alone is ludicrous. I would not be at all surprised if one day we discover that we have been guided through our history by foreign influences far beyond our current comprehension."

EPILOGUE

The questioner had stepped forward while Daniel had been talking to reveal himself.

Before Daniel stood a small, slightly built, almost frail, boyish male with blond hair, and a prominent forehead. But the most outstanding feature was his bright blue eyes, they were large, upturned and piercing. His smile was innocent and wise and Daniel instantly realized he had met this person before. Daniel's own eyes widened in recognition and his look of astonishment broadened into a welcoming grin.

Over the next few days, the Jameses, along with their reunited son, had put together the story they would tell the world about Alexander, as they had chosen to call him. He was adopted from an orphanage in Eastern Europe. They had kept it secret because they were not sure it would go through and did not want to get their hopes up. Though a little suspicious Sidd did not question Daniel closely on the matter. But the fact was Alexander James looked and acted quite different from any child he had ever met, foreign or not.

Saturday afternoon and for the first time Daniel and Melanie were taking Alex to meet the rest of the Sharma clan.

As Sidd welcomed them into the foyer, Jezebel, their black Labrador, raced like a watchdog from the kitchen at the back of the house. Sidd made a desperate grab for her fearing she would hurt the diminutive boy, but she slipped through his grasp and stopped short to nuzzle Alex, whimpering affectionately. Relieved, Sidd quickly ushered them into the recreation room where Deepa was feeding two-and-a-half-year-old Kamala in her highchair. Deepa rose to meet them, as Kamala, whining and squirming wildly, tried to get out of the chair. Clearly something had upset her tremendously. Thwarted by her tray and restraints she struggled in vain and then burst into sobs of frustration.

Deepa hoisted her up and out but still Kamala writhed in her arms until Sidd advised, "She wants down, Dee." Deepa set her on the floor with the comforting words, "It's all right, honey, Alex is our friend." But instead of running away from the visitors as all expected, little Kamala ran across the floor toward Alex as fast as her stumbling young "sea legs" could carry her and, to the astonishment of all, literally fell into his arms. As the two children embraced like long departed siblings, Sidd quipped, "I'd say she likes him!"

Daniel, though, had been taking in the little drama with clearer understanding, and to his own surprise and the consternation of all, blurted out, "I think they've met."

His observation would have far reaching implications for the small group in that rec room…and the world.